"Is that why you have a scar on your jaw?"

He slid Selena a look. Her gaze was on the road in front of them, but the scar was faint these days. Hardly noticeable. Unless someone had been looking.

Which, of course, he knew she had. Four years they'd worked in the same department. He was aware there was...chemistry. It was why he kept his distance. Clearly he had enough of his own baggage—he didn't need to add the complication of romantic entanglements.

Still, he wasn't unaffected that she'd looked.

"Yeah. The guy shot me, but mostly missed. Didn't have time to check I was dead before he ran."

"And they caught him? The FBI?"

"Before he'd even gotten out of the neighborhood."

D0037020

HUNTING
A KILLER

NICOLE HELM

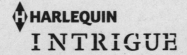

For all those happily-ever-afters that started as
workplace romances.

Special thanks and acknowledgment are given to Nicole Helm for
her contribution to the Tactical Crime Division:
Traverse City miniseries.

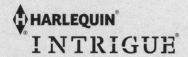

Recycling programs
for this product may
not exist in your area.

ISBN-13: 978-1-335-40152-6

Hunting a Killer

Copyright © 2021 by Harlequin Books S.A.

For questions and comments about the quality of this book,
please contact us at CustomerService@Harlequin.com.

Harlequin Enterprises ULC
22 Adelaide St. West, 40th Floor
Toronto, Ontario M5H 4E3, Canada
www.Harlequin.com

Printed in U.S.A.

Nicole Helm grew up with her nose in a book and the dream of one day becoming a writer. Luckily, after a few failed career choices, she gets to follow that dream—writing down-to-earth contemporary romance and romantic suspense. From farmers to cowboys, Midwest to *the* West, Nicole writes stories about people finding themselves and finding love in the process. She lives in Missouri with her husband and two sons and dreams of someday owning a barn.

Books by Nicole Helm

Harlequin Intrigue

Hunting a Killer

A Badlands Cops Novel

South Dakota Showdown
Covert Complication
Backcountry Escape
Isolated Threat
Badlands Beware
Close Range Christmas

Carsons & Delaneys:
Battle Tested

Wyoming Cowboy Marine
Wyoming Cowboy Sniper
Wyoming Cowboy Ranger
Wyoming Cowboy Bodyguard

Carsons & Delaneys

Wyoming Cowboy Justice
Wyoming Cowboy Protection
Wyoming Christmas Ransom

Stone Cold Texas Ranger
Stone Cold Undercover Agent
Stone Cold Christmas Ranger

Harlequin Superromance

A Farmers' Market Story

All I Have
All I Am
All I Want

Falling for the New Guy
Too Friendly to Date
Too Close to Resist

Visit the Author Profile page at Harlequin.com.

CAST OF CHARACTERS

Axel Morrow—Supervisory special agent with the FBI's Tactical Crime Division, working with Selena Lopez to track three escaped convicts.

Selena Lopez—Special agent K-9 handler with the FBI's Tactical Crime Division, working with Axel to track and apprehend the escaped convicts, one of whom she's related to.

Blanca—Selena's K-9 companion.

Opaline Lopez—Selena's sister and TCD's tech guru. The two sisters don't get along.

Peter Lopez—Selena and Opaline's half brother. He's on the run with two dangerous criminals.

Aria Calletti—Rookie to TCD, helping catch the escaped convicts.

Dr. Carly Welsh—Member of the TCD team helping catch the escaped convicts.

Max McRay—Special agent with TCD, helping catch the escaped convicts.

Alana Suzuki—Director of TCD.

Rihanna Clark—TCD member acting as liaison with local police as TCD tracks the escaped convicts.

Prologue

The tears leaked out of Kay Duvall's eyes, even as she tried to focus on what she had to do. *Had* to do to bring Ben home safe.

She fumbled with her ID and punched in the code that would open the side door, usually only used by a guard taking a smoke break. It would be easy for the men behind her to escape from this side of the prison.

It went against everything she was supposed to do. Everything she considered right and good.

A quiet sob escaped her lips. They had her son. How could she not help them escape? Nothing mattered beyond her son's life.

"Would you stop already?" one of the prisoners muttered. He'd made her give him her gun, which he now jabbed into her back. "Crying isn't going to change anything. So just shut up."

She didn't care so much about her own life, or if she'd be fired. She didn't care what happened to her as long as they let her son go. So she swallowed down the sobs and blinked out as many tears as she could, hoping to stem the tide of them.

She got the door open and slid out first—because the man holding the gun pushed it into her back until she moved forward.

They moved out the door behind her, dressed in the clothes she'd stolen from the locker room and Lost and Found. Anything warm she could get her hands on to help them escape into the frigid February night.

Help them escape. Help three dangerous men escape prison. When she was supposed to keep them inside.

It didn't matter anymore. She just wanted them gone. If they were gone, they'd let her baby go. They had to let her baby go.

Kay forced her legs to move, one foot in front of the other, toward the gate she could unlock without setting off any alarms. She unlocked it, steadier this time if only because she kept thinking once they were gone she could get in contact with Ben.

She flung open the gate and gestured them out into the parking lot. "Stay out of the safety lights and no one should bug you."

"You better hope not," one of the men growled.

"The minute you sound that alarm, your kid is dead. You got it?" This one was the ringleader. The one who'd been in for murder. Who else would he kill out there in the world?

Guilt pooled in Kay's belly, but she had to ignore it. She had to live with it. Whatever guilt she'd felt would be survivable. Living without her son wouldn't be. Besides, she had to believe they'd be caught. They'd do something else terrible and be caught.

As long as her son was alive, she didn't care.

The three men disappeared into the night, wearing the clothes she'd stolen for them. She hoped they froze to death. She hoped every bad thing befell them. As soon as her baby was safe, she'd help the authorities in whatever way she could.

She slammed the gate closed and locked it. She was sick with anger and terror, and her hands shook as she fumbled for her phone. She dialed her mother. Just because she couldn't sound the alarm didn't mean she couldn't make sure Mom was all right. Had they hurt her when they'd kidnapped Ben? Was she terrified too?

Or worse, dead? Mom definitely would have fought off anyone trying to take Ben, even if it ended her life.

Another sob escaped Kay's mouth, followed by a bigger, louder one when her mother answered sounding perfectly calm and cheerful. "Hi, honey."

She could only gasp for breath. Relief but new fears bubbling up inside her.

"What on Earth is wrong?" her mother asked, worry and confusion seeping into her tone. *New* worry. *New* confusion.

Kay blinked, taken aback by how calm her mom sounded. Did she not know? Had Ben been kidnapped without Mom even realizing? How could that happen?

"Ben…" she managed to croak.

"Shoveling in his mac and cheese like usual. We really need to work on getting this boy some vegetables.

I know you don't want to give him a complex, but he can't subsist on cheese and pasta alone. Are you okay?"

"I'm fine. Mom… Everything is okay there? You're sure."

"Of course I'm sure. Ben's right here. Did you want to talk to him? Ben, here's your mom."

She closed her eyes, tears pouring over her cheeks. She heard her baby's voice, safe as could be, chattering about something in the background. She swallowed down the sinking, horrible realization she was a stupid, utter failure. "No, Mom," she croaked. "I have to go. I may be home late."

Her mother's words were little more than a buzz as she hung up the phone and slid it back into her pocket.

There was only one thing to do now—sound the alarm, own up to her mistake and pray she didn't end up an inmate herself.

Chapter One

Selena Lopez yawned as she filed into the meeting room of the Tactical Crime Division—a specialized FBI team made up of experts from several active divisions in one small group.

Selena's specialization was currently back home asleep in her crate. Lucky dog. Of course, if Selena was deployed into the field, she'd be waking her German shepherd and taking her out to track regardless of the time.

She yawned again. She was used to middle-of-the-night calls, going on little to no sleep, but her neighbors had been having one hell of a party. *Again.*

She was really getting tired of apartment living.

In the boardroom, half the team were in various states of disarray already situated around the large table. Sleep-tumbled hair, casual clothes and desperate looks at the cups of coffee in front of them were all typical signs of a middle of the night call.

Selena knew once their director walked into the

room, they'd all sharpen into the tools they were. But for a few more minutes they could be human.

Axel Morrow walked in behind her. He looked like he'd somehow had the time to take a shower, comb his hair and get dressed in fresh clothes without a wrinkle in sight. Casual though the jeans and long-sleeved tee were, he could have walked in at two in the afternoon looking like that. His blond hair didn't appear sleep-tousled at all, and his green eyes were perfectly alert.

How did he look perfect at two o'clock in the morning? When she knew he'd driven in farther than everyone else, since he lived on an old nonoperating farm outside town.

She frowned at him when he took the seat next to her. God, he smelled good. And when he flashed her a smile, that obnoxious fluttering she got whenever she saw him spread deeper and flirted way too close with serious attraction.

Which was *not* allowed.

She knew exactly where those kind of thoughts led. To poor choices and embarrassing breakups. The TCD team was pretty tight-knit, and she wouldn't jeopardize her good standing here over attraction. Not when everyone liked her.

She glanced at her sister across the table. Okay, maybe not everyone. Opaline had been here longer. She hadn't exactly been hostile toward Selena joining the group, but she hadn't been welcoming either. Their continued standoff remained as it always was.

Tense and mostly silent. But they worked together when they had to.

Selena had hoped coming here might help bridge the gap between them, but she'd yet to figure out *how*. They were so different. What they believed and how they felt about their family... How could it not keep them at odds?

Dr. Carly Welsh entered the room and sat down on the other side of her. "You look rough."

Selena slid her friend a look. "You try living in party city. I bet they aren't even allowed to have parties in your swank place, and I'm guessing Noah's isn't prone to loud raves into the night."

Carly rolled her eyes, but the smile she always got when anyone mentioned her fiancé spread across her face. "You could live somewhere nicer," she pointed out.

"Who's got the time to find a nice place when we're getting called in at two in the morning?"

Carly didn't answer because Alana Suzuki walked in. Director of TCD, she looked put together in her smart suit. It didn't matter that it was the middle of the night. She carried a folder, and her face was grim.

Which made Selena fidget. Alana was *all* business, and while their business was serious, there was something...discomfiting about the way Alana specifically looked at her.

Then Opaline.

"Selena, Opaline, could I see you outside for a moment?"

The discomfort settled into full-on dread in her gut, but she got to her feet and walked out of the boardroom with Opaline.

Alana stopped in the hallway and looked at both of them with some sympathy. "I wish we had more time so that I could put this delicately."

"No need," Selena replied, careful to keep her voice even and calm. "Lay it on us."

She heard her sister huff, but Selena couldn't look at her just now. She had to keep it together. Doing her job required being able to compartmentalize. Opaline had never understood the fine art of pushing things away, let alone dealing with things at appropriate moments. She always reacted. Oftentimes when it got both of them in more trouble.

"I'm afraid you have a personal connection to this assignment," Alana began.

Selena closed her eyes. She knew she couldn't outwardly react, but in this moment, just the three of them, she gave herself a moment to breathe. "Peter."

When Selena opened her eyes, Alana's expression was empathetic. "Yes, your brother has escaped prison with two other convicts. We need to stop them before they cross the Canadian border."

Alana was a good boss, an excellent director. The perfect mix of personal and business. She knew how to take care of her people. Selena appreciated that beyond measure.

Which meant she wouldn't let Peter jeopardize her job here. She'd do whatever she had to do to complete the mission that involved her half brother. She'd bring him to justice, no matter what it took.

"We'll go over the details inside, but before we head in there, I wanted to give you both a chance to bow out. We can replace either or both of you for this mission if you feel your relationship with Peter would keep you from being able to do your job. Conversely, you can take some time to think about—"

"I don't need any time," Selena said, keeping her voice devoid of any and all emotion, no matter how it battered at her on the inside. "If we're tracking, you need me and Blanca."

Alana nodded, then turned to Selena's sister. "Opaline?"

Selena finally glanced at her. Opaline looked at her like she was some kind of monster. She'd never understood you couldn't save people who didn't want to be saved. And seemed to blame Selena for the fact their half brother did not want to be saved.

"I can handle it," Opaline said, glaring daggers at Selena. Her voice was rough, and her eyes were bright with unshed tears.

For a half brother they hardly knew, who'd refused help, again and again. Whose very existence had caused such a rift in their family, it still hadn't healed.

Selena would never understand it or Opaline. She turned on a heel and walked back into the boardroom. No one looked directly at her, but she could feel their consideration all the same.

She slid into her chair, keeping her expression neutral. Carly was friend enough not to say anything, but of course Axel would be obnoxious.

"You okay?" Axel asked.

Selena raised her chin, keeping her gaze on where Alana was taking her place at the head of the board-room table. "Just fine."

SELENA WAS DEFINITELY not just fine, but as Alana walked back into the boardroom, Axel Morrow had to focus on the task at hand. TCD business, and the challenge Alana Suzuki would lay out before them.

"Team, I appreciate you all coming in at such an hour, but we need to get started as soon as possible. Opaline?"

Where Selena was completely blank, Opaline was outwardly shaken by whatever Alana had told them. It didn't take a special agent to deduce whatever the mission was involved the sisters on some kind of personal level.

Still, Opaline went to the front of the room and took over the computer. As the tech specialist for TCD, it was always her job to run through the slideshow.

"Three inmates have escaped a maximum-security federal prison this evening. Because of the nature of their crimes, the way they've escaped and where we think they're going, TCD has been tasked with stopping them and bringing them back before they cross the border to Canada. Police have set up roadblocks on routes to the border since they likely stole a car, but so far, no sightings to give us an idea of their route."

Alana nodded at Opaline, who brought up a mug shot on the screen at the front of the room.

"Leonard Koch is the presumed leader of this little trio. He's in for life for the murder of a family, among a litany of other charges."

Alana didn't look directly at Axel, but he felt the consideration all the same. Murder was part and parcel with his job as special agent, even in his supervisory role. He still considered himself part of the team more than some kind of leader.

But the murder of a family was…well, it hit close to home. Families being murdered was why he was here. As an FBI agent, as the person he was today. To stop men like Leonard Koch before he hurt any more people.

Alana nodded at the screen, and the mug shot changed to the next slide, which included a list of charges.

Max McRay, special agent and explosives expert, let out a low whistle next to him. "That's quite a rap sheet. How'd this guy get out?"

"He and his cohorts convinced a prison guard they had her son. Unfortunately, since they had a lot of personal information and were threatening her son's life, she fell for it. On the bright side, the child is fine. So, right now we're just focused on apprehension." Alana pointed at Opaline to bring up the next slide.

"Steve Jenson is our number two. A history of battery, assault, but he's in for his role in an armed burglary that went south when a security guard was killed in the resulting shootout. Though we don't have any concrete idea of what kind of access they have to supplies, we're considering them both armed and extremely dangerous."

"And the third?" Aria Calletti asked. She was the newest member of TCD, but she'd proven herself extraordinarily capable last year when she'd been instrumental in bringing down a murderous smuggling ring. Axel had been with her when she'd gotten their best lead to talk. She was a go-getter, that was for sure.

But Axel wished she hadn't pressed so quickly when it clearly upset Opaline. The woman let out a shaky sigh before she brought up the next picture.

"The third escapee is Peter Lopez," Alana said with more gravity than she'd used to announce the other two.

As it was a group of highly trained FBI agents, no one immediately looked to Selena or Opaline, but that didn't mean everyone in the room wasn't paying attention to the reactions to the two women who shared a last name with the third man.

Opaline wiped at her eyes and shook her head. Meanwhile, a surreptitious look at Selena showed a woman with no reaction at all.

"Peter is Opaline and Selena's brother, and they've both been briefed in advance and given the option to remove themselves if they felt like they couldn't do their jobs, but both agreed to stay on."

"We're not close," Selena said, her voice even. "He's our half brother, the product of an affair our father had. Don't feel like you have to walk on eggshells around me. We might share some genetic material, but I don't know the guy."

Alana nodded, and Opaline glared daggers at her sister, but she didn't argue with the assessment.

Axel found he wasn't sure which reaction made more sense. The complete lack of emotion had to be hiding *something*, but if they were so removed from the man, why was Opaline so upset?

Something he'd get to the bottom of before the day was out, but for now, they had to decide on a course of action.

"Opaline, would you bring up the map?"

The screen changed from Peter's mug shot to a topographical map of the area between the prison in northern Michigan and the Canadian border.

"We have reason to believe they're heading for Canada. We want to catch them before they do, and before they hurt anyone. The first wave of that will fall to Selena."

Selena nodded. "I'll take Blanca up to the prison and we'll start from there. Unless we have new known whereabouts?"

"Rihanna will keep in close touch with local authorities," Alana said, referring to TCD's police and press liaison. "If we get any updates on location, that will be relayed to you and Axel."

Selena straightened next to him. "Axel?"

"He'll partner with you on this. No one works alone. Aria and Carly will work together as well, and we'll bring in Scott Fletcher from the FBI to pair with Max to keep things even. We'll station the teams of two along the Canadian border. While Selena and Axel track, you'll set up a perimeter where hopefully if they don't catch up to the trio, you guys can stop them. You'll want to stay in close contact, and adjust as necessary. Axel will be lead on this."

He nodded at Alana before sliding Selena a look. She continued to show absolutely no reaction. She was a statue.

"We might be in charge of tracking," Alana said, "but the local police will be helpful resources, especially if the escapees cause any trouble in some of the smaller towns or more remote areas. This is a true team effort. The six of you tracking, Opaline working on tech—she'll get you all the maps you'll want to download onto your phones. Rihanna is working with local authorities in case we catch wind of them somewhere. No one acts alone."

"And we bring them all in before anyone else is killed," Axel added. Maybe it didn't need to be said, but there was an urgency that had to be heeded. He stood as Selena did.

"I'll follow you to your apartment in the Jeep. We'll go from there."

She didn't say anything, just gave the slightest nod and then walked out the door. Axel looked back at Alana, but her expression was neutral.

This wouldn't be as simple as bringing three fugitives to justice, that much was for sure.

Chapter Two

Selena pulled her personal car into the parking space of her apartment complex. The partiers seemed to have finally dispersed—since it was nearing four in the morning at this point.

She trudged up the stairs to her top-floor apartment and thought about Carly saying she could move if she didn't like where she was. Selena was sure there wasn't time, nor did she have the energy to look for a new place. But she realized she'd been doing this for four years now. Saying she didn't have time. Saying she didn't have the energy.

Was she going to settle into this crappy apartment complex forever and just exist? She put a lot into her work at TCD, and enjoyed it, but that didn't mean the rest of her life had to be…this.

She shook her head as she unlocked her door and then the dead bolt she'd installed herself. There really *wasn't* time to deal with her living quarters right now—but she promised herself when this assignment was over, she'd really start looking into a more permanent living space.

For now, the focus had to be getting her dog and tracking the three escapees.

One of whom you know.

Didn't matter. She hadn't lied to her team and friends. She'd had limited contact with Peter. She'd tried to help him over the years. Not because she'd wanted to, but because her father had insisted her position in law enforcement made her the perfect person to reach his son.

His son. With a woman who had not been his wife at the time. Yet he'd expected Selena to step in and…

Selena couldn't let herself go down these messy emotional paths. She'd attended Peter's trial in some silly attempt to understand how a man related to her could go so wrong, and what she'd realized sitting there watching him answer questions belligerently was that she couldn't allow herself to take responsibility for her father's mistakes. Or Peter's.

She'd been in the midst of her own stupid personal drama, surprised at all the ways she could screw up her own life. All the ways she could fail.

Then and there she'd promised herself to stop letting other people run her life. She wouldn't feel guilty about Peter, she wouldn't keep helping her father when she didn't want to and she certainly wouldn't let herself get so wrapped up in a man that her entire career could be threatened.

No, she'd come to a lot of conclusions in that courtroom. Her life was her own. Peter being involved in this latest suspect apprehension was irrelevant. Partnering with Axel Morrow? Irrelevant.

Selena walked into her bedroom. Blanca raised her head with a huff.

"Sorry to disturb, queen of the manor, but we've got work to do." Selena opened her closet and grabbed the backpack she always had ready to go should she be called off on a mission.

At the word *work*, Blanca slowly got to her feet, stretched and then shook her head. She padded out of the room, and while Selena gathered the rest of her stuff, she could hear Blanca lapping up some water.

Satisfied she had as much as was reasonable to take, Selena headed to the kitchen and grabbed herself a water bottle and a protein bar. There wouldn't be time for breakfast.

Blanca waited by the door. Selena took a moment to pause, to pull herself together. Axel was…a problem, but she could hardly let him know that. She knelt next to her dog.

"This isn't going to be an easy one." She scratched Blanca behind the ears and glanced out the window that looked out over the parking lot. Axel was pulling the Jeep into a parking space next to her car. She sighed. "And we've got help."

She couldn't be bitter about it. Working alone was rarely part and parcel with this kind of mission. She might have preferred Carly's company, or even Aria, rookie though she was.

Okay, in her apartment she could be honest with herself. She'd prefer anyone over Axel. Even her sister, probably. She might get in a fight with her sister, but she wouldn't have to deal with…attraction.

Even when they didn't have a mission to complete, she didn't want to think about that enduring problem with Axel Morrow. "So aren't you lucky you have more important things to concern yourself with?" she muttered to herself.

She stood and grabbed the duffel by the door that had all Blanca's supplies. Axel was waiting at the Jeep, which she appreciated. Selena let Blanca out then focused on locking up the apartment. When she made her way down the stairs, Blanca was sniffing around the grass while Axel stood next to the Jeep.

Watching her, not the dog.

She didn't let the jolt inside her show on the outside. It was still dark. The only light illuminating him was from the parking lot light. Still, his gaze on her felt electric.

She let out a slow breath, being careful to keep her expression neutral as she approached. "Gassed up?"

"All ready to head out to the prison," Axel confirmed.

Selena tossed her bags into the back of the Jeep, next to Axel's bag. A beat-up military pack. She whistled for Blanca, who trotted up to Axel.

He offered the dog a pat, then opened the back door for her. Blanca jumped in. At six, she was a veteran and a pro. She knew her job, and she did it well. She'd acclimated to TCD quicker than Selena herself had, but four years later, it often felt like they'd always worked with TCD.

"I'll drive."

As if she had any doubt Mr. Second in Command would drive and call the shots. Much as she respected Axel on a professional level, she was going to have to bite her tongue to keep from knee-jerk sniping at him on a personal one.

Hardly his fault she thought he was hot. Definitely not his fault she'd already learned her lesson in that department. She moved into the passenger seat without a word.

He climbed into the driver's seat and turned the key in the ignition. Blanca had already settled herself into the back—specially designed for tactical dogs, so Blanca wouldn't be too jostled by any off-terrain driving.

"No word on any new sightings?" Selena asked, pulling out her phone and bringing up the map of the area Opaline had sent all members of the team. By the time they got to the prison, the escapees would have a significant head start. They could head toward the prison, but what they really needed was someone to report seeing the fugitives.

"Afraid not," Axel said pulling out of her apartment complex's parking lot.

"I don't know how we're going to catch up with them at this rate."

"I imagine they'll hang low during the day. They

won't want to be spotted—not before they cross the border. That should give us a few hours to minimize the distance. There's only so many ways to get to Canada, and the prison guard was sure that's where they were headed."

Selena wasn't so sure. There wasn't much in terms of towns or people between the prison and the Canadian border. Lots and lots of wilderness and lakes, though. The kind it was easy to disappear into. Even crossing by water could be done with the right amount of money. They might not have had any leading the prison, but that didn't mean some wasn't waiting for them.

They drove for a while. Selena was grateful Axel didn't try to fill the silence with chatter. He was good at knowing when to do that and when not to. He read people well.

It was one of the many reasons she avoided being alone with him. The last thing she needed was him *reading* all that went on in her head when she looked at him.

Axel's phone rang, and he used the Jeep's Bluetooth system to answer it. "Morrow."

"Hey, guys," Rihanna's voice greeted them. "I just got off the phone with local police in Winston. There's been an incident, and it looks to be our guys."

"What happened?" Axel demanded. With a glance at the lane next to him, he moved over to get off at the exit, immediately altering their course to head toward Winston instead of the prison.

Selena studied her map, but Rihanna's pause on the

other end had her gut clenching in dread as she calculated their new driving distance and how much of a head start the escapees had.

"Local wildlife officers found two poachers who'd been shot," Rihanna said at last. "One was capable of telling local law enforcement a little about who'd shot him. They'd stumbled upon three men, who fired without pause. They left our witness for dead after stealing guns and money. His description of them matches our escapees."

Axel's grip on the steering wheel tightened. "You said one was capable of talking to law enforcement," he said, his voice abnormally cold. "What about the other poacher?"

Again, Rihanna paused, and Selena watched Axel's expression get harder…and harder. She wasn't sure why he cared about the other poacher. Another set of eyes? Two stories instead of one? More witnesses meant more information and—

"He was dead when the wildlife officers arrived."

The coldness in his voice spread into his gaze on the road. The clear *fury* pumping off him was an emotional response Selena wouldn't have expected from him. He was always so controlled. So *cool* under pressure.

"Get us the location," he said, the words having a sharp bite. "We'll meet local law enforcement there."

"I'll make sure they know you're coming." Rihanna hung up.

Axel increased the speed of the Jeep. The roads were mostly empty this early in the morning, but he was taking exits too fast, and curves even faster, to the point Selena was actually afraid they'd wreck before they got where they needed to be.

"Getting there faster won't change the fact the man is dead," Selena said, gripping the handle of the door as tight as she could.

"But it might stop another innocent man from being killed."

THOUGH IT GRATED, Axel slowed down. It was possible he was pushing things just a little too hard. Yes, it was a failure a man had been killed. A failure he felt deep in his bones. But if he did something foolish because of that feeling of failure, that would also be his fault.

And if it hurt Selena or Blanca…well, no. He had to get a hold of himself. They'd get to Winston soon enough.

"I don't like being too late," he muttered, the closest to an apology he was going to get.

"Who does?" Selena replied, too flippantly for his tastes. "But I can't blame myself for every criminal who does the wrong thing. I'd never get out of bed in the morning."

Axel knew he had to control his emotions, knew he couldn't compare this to all those years ago, but his temper strained at how unaffected she was. "Even your own brother's wrong thing? Because I think that'd mean *something* to you."

She whipped her gaze toward him. There was fury

in her dark eyes, but she'd paled a bit. Like he'd landed a blow.

Hell. He'd screwed up. He could blame it on lack of sleep or what have you, but the bottom line was he should handle loss of life better. He had to. "I'm sorry. That was uncalled for."

She slowly looked away from him, her eyes on the road before them. The sun was flirting with the horizon, and she said nothing. Not that it was okay. Not that she accepted his apology. Not even telling him where he could shove his apology.

Which was somehow worse. He squeezed the steering wheel, then forced himself to loosen his grip. "Look. It bothers me."

More silence, because it bothering him was hardly an excuse for being a jerk.

"Which isn't an excuse. I can't excuse it. I shouldn't have said it. I shouldn't have let the emotional response take over. But I've been the survivor in that situation, so there *is* an emotional response. Better to get it out now rather than let it bubble up later." Or so he'd tell himself for the time being so he could focus on getting the job done.

Selena's eyebrows drew together. "I don't remember hearing anything about that."

"Not on duty. Not… I was a kid."

Her silence in response made his skin feel too tight. While there were members of the team who knew about his past, he didn't trot it out to discuss for fun. If people knew, fine, but he'd rather not have to get into it too often.

Still, he'd been the jerk. This was his penance.

"My family was killed when I was seven. The FBI had been after the guy for months and were closing in, but they didn't make it in time. He killed my parents, my brother. He shot me, but by that time they'd surrounded the house. I was transported in enough time to save my life. I got into this so some kid didn't have to be the one with the murdered family members, and yeah, I can't save everyone. But I don't like to lose a life on an active case I'm on, knowing if we hadn't sat around in a briefing meeting we might have gotten there."

"I don't know what to. say," Selena said softly. "I guess there really isn't anything to say."

Most people said they were sorry, which he hated. Or went on and on about how awful it must have been. How brave he was to survive it. To go into the FBI. He appreciated the fact she knew there wasn't anything that would actually help.

"Except briefing is necessary to know who, how and what. We could have been on the road to the prison sooner, but it wouldn't have saved that guy's life."

Axel pushed out a breath. "I guess not."

"There's enough hard stuff in this job without heaping guilt and blame on yourself or your team that doesn't belong there. You start questioning—"

"I'm not questioning. I have the utmost confidence in our team."

"Okay, well…" Both their phones pinged at the same time. He let Selena deal with the information.

"We're meeting the local police force at a cabin near where the incident took place," Selena said, tapping a few keys on her phone. "GPS isn't going to be much help once we go off-road, so I'll navigate once we're in Winston."

Axel nodded wordlessly. He was glad they were moving on. They had a job to do, not pasts to obsess over.

"Is that why you have a scar on your jaw?"

He slid Selena a look. Her gaze was on the road in front of them, but the scar was faint these days. Hardly noticeable. Unless someone had been looking.

Which of course, he knew she had. Four years they'd worked in the same department. He was aware there was…chemistry. It was why he kept his distance. Clearly he had enough of his own baggage, he didn't need to add the complication of romantic entanglements.

Still, he wasn't *unaffected* that she looked.

"Yeah. The guy shot me, but mostly missed. Didn't have time to check I was dead before he ran."

"And they caught him? The FBI?"

"Before he'd even gotten out of the neighborhood."

"That's rough." She shifted in the seat and slid her arm back to give Blanca a pet, all the while keeping her gaze on the road. "Turn here," she instructed. "We want to go in on the west side of town."

Axel only nodded and took the turn she instructed him to make.

"I got into law enforcement because of family too. Because of Peter, to be specific. Some part of me thought if I became a cop, I'd be able to talk him out of being hell-bent on destroying his own life."

"I thought you didn't have a relationship."

"We don't. Doesn't mean I wasn't aware what was going on with him. Mom complaining about Dad's deadbeat son. Dad washing his hands of any kind of trouble because heaven forbid he try to help his own kid." She shrugged jerkily. "Point is, we've all got our stuff, right? Sometimes it pops up and gets the best of us for a minute or two, but we're pros. I've never seen you falter when it mattered. I haven't either."

She was saying it so he didn't think too much about the moment before. That was obvious, but he thought she was saying it a bit for herself too. She might act un-affected, but Peter meant something to her. They both had their baggage that might affect them as they went through the assignment.

But in the end, regardless of feelings of failure or brotherly attachment, they'd both do their jobs.

They had to.

Chapter Three

Early morning light filtered through the trees as Selena followed Axel toward the flashing lights of a police car and the low hum of conversation. She held Blanca on her leash, keeping her close.

The air was frigid, and Selena was grateful for the thick tactical boots she wore as they hiked through the snow. It was packed down from many sets of footprints. Were any of them her brother's?

It didn't matter. She couldn't think of Peter like her brother. She had to think about what he really was: a stranger she was tasked with bringing to justice. She didn't know him. And he most certainly didn't know her.

So, he was a stranger. She would work with Axel to apprehend him, because regardless of what genes they shared, he was responsible for killing a man. Maybe he hadn't pulled the trigger on the poor poacher who'd come across the wrong men at the wrong time.

But maybe he had.

Axel's strides were long, and she didn't bother trying to keep up. Blanca sniffed the snow and trees and oriented herself to her new surroundings—in order for her to be ready to track, she needed that time. Selena refused to admit she was giving the time to herself, as well.

She needed a little distance from Axel Morrow. She hadn't gotten into the FBI and this special unit by being soft, by showing compassion and empathy for her partner. There wasn't time for that. A teammate had to be understanding and forgive their partner's mistakes, or you'd never keep moving forward.

But that wasn't what she'd done. She'd given him a piece of herself. When he'd apologized for snapping at her and using her brother to do it, she should have accepted it. The end.

But *no*. She'd had to tell him she'd gotten into law enforcement because of Peter. She'd *shared*, when she knew that was professional suicide as a woman in a tough field. Oh, she'd worked with Axel long enough to know he wasn't one of those guys who used every weakness a woman showed against her, but that didn't change the fact she was on dangerous ground.

Dangerous ground she'd walked on before, and lost far too much of herself in the process.

By the time she caught up with Axel, he was already deep in conversation with the local police officer.

"I think they'd planned to stay at this cabin for the day," the officer was saying. He gave Selena and Blanca a brief nod. "But the poachers came in and… Well, you can read the statement."

"I'd like to talk to the survivor first, if you don't mind."

Again, the officer nodded. "We've got him in the car. We've already taken his statement, and we'll drive him home once things are good on your end."

The officer started walking toward the police cruiser, but Selena stopped Axel with a light touch of the arm. It would be impossible to get through this mission without touching him like this—lightly, casually—but that didn't mean she had to like it.

"I'm going to search the cabin," she said, maybe a little bit sharper and more authoritatively than she needed to.

His expression was flat. She'd worked with him for four years, and she'd learned—whether she wanted to or not—to read Axel's moods on a case. The murder bothered him, plain and simple, and now she knew why.

She wished she didn't.

"Cops said they left everything as is," Axel said quietly, his green eyes searching the woods around them. "Blanca should be able to pick up something. We'll track from here with her."

"We shouldn't take too much time. The snow will make tracking harder, and they've already got a head start."

"Yeah, but this poacher might have overheard something. Search the house while I talk to him. We'll head out from there as soon as we can."

They parted in silent agreement, and Selena urged Blanca to the cabin. Since she had winter gloves on, she opened the door and stepped inside. There was no electricity, and very few windows, so the interior lighting was dim at best. She pulled the flashlight off her utility belt and began to search.

"Stay," she ordered the dog. Blanca settled into a seated position by the door while Selena moved forward.

They couldn't have been here long, and Selena had to wonder why they'd rest at night. Wouldn't they want to get as far away from the jail as possible? On foot, they hadn't gotten more than twenty miles from the prison. Which meant they hadn't stolen a car.

Yet.

It had been cold last night. Temperatures dipping well below zero. Even if they'd stolen some supplies, they wouldn't be well equipped for a trek across the northern Michigan wilderness in February. Maybe they hadn't stopped because they'd wanted to, but because they simply hadn't been prepared for what lay in front of them.

But the escape had been so well planned, executed perfectly. Why had they decided to escape in the dead of winter? What more was at stake here aside from simply freedom?

Too many questions. It wasn't her job to imagine answers. It was her job to find facts to bring them to answers. Or if not answers, the men themselves.

Selena let her flashlight roam the area of the small, rustic cabin. It was sparse. Clearly a space used simply as a base for hunting or fishing in the wilderness rather than any kind of cozy vacation home. There were quite a lot of these types of cabins in the area the police had been searching. Hunting spaces, or the nicer lake houses probably closed up for the winter, family cabins. If they knew where to look, the escapees would be able to find shelter here and there. Most of it empty in the middle of February.

But this one hadn't been. On first sweep, she saw nothing in the main area. There was a couch, a table and a fireplace to one side, and then a kitchenette to the other. There was one door besides the front door, which Selena assumed was a bathroom. If anyone slept here, they likely slept on the couch or on the floor.

Selena wrinkled her nose at the floor. It was hard planks of wood, no carpet or rugs to soften anything up. This wouldn't be the place she'd want to spend some free hours.

The windows had thick curtains that looked like they'd been collecting dust for years. She approached the fireplace. Though there was no fire, not even a glow of embers, she could smell the trace of smoke in the air. When she squatted to hold her hand over the blackened wood, the air was warmer than it had been closer to the door.

They'd come in here. Made themselves comfortable, then been surprised into moving again.

Selena glanced back at the door. Blanca still sat dutifully, waiting for the order. But if Selena didn't find anything that might have a good scent on it, there wouldn't be much for Blanca to go on. They'd have to get a look at the tracks outside and make a decision from there.

Selena got back to her feet, and as she stood she noticed something slightly different colored than the blackened wood in the hearth. A gray fabric. She leaned closer. It looked like a glove.

There was no way to tell whether it belonged to one of the men they were searching for, or the owner of the cabin, or another passerby altogether. But it was *something*.

"Blanca. Come."

AXEL PRIDED HIMSELF on the fine art of compartmentalizing. Senseless murder always tested that ability, but he muscled through because that was what this job required of him.

He loved his job. The structure. The clear goal. Sometimes cases dealt more in the gray area, but when it came to murder, the task was clear—stop the murderer before he could do any more damage.

Axel frowned at the surviving poacher. There was more to his story he wasn't telling. Axel slid a look at the cop next to him. From what Axel could tell, he was a good one. But tired and ready for this to be over.

Axel couldn't blame him. Even with the sun inching up in the sky, it was bitterly cold. The snow was fairly deep, and despite waterproof clothing, the chill of having your feet surrounded by snow wasn't for the faint of heart.

The poacher sat in the back seat of the cruiser with

the door open. He looked at his hands. When he answered Axel's questions, questions the cop had already asked him before they'd gotten here, he mumbled.

Axel nodded away from the cruiser, and the officer followed him. "I want five minutes alone with him."

The officer scratched his cheek and sighed. "Poor guy's friend is dead and he's been out here for hours. Let me take him in."

"He's got more information than he's letting on. Come on. You know he's afraid of the poaching repercussions."

"I've told him—"

"Just give me five minutes alone. That's all."

The officer sighed but gave a short nod and then moved stiffly away. Axel turned back to the poacher. He'd said he didn't know which way the escapees had gone. That they hadn't taken anything.

"What aren't you telling us?"

The man looked up, noted the cop had moved away. Still, he shrugged. "Nothing I can think of."

"Your buddy is dead, and it's my job to stop these guys from killing anyone else. The local's gone. Anything you tell me? Stays between us. Whatever illegal hunting you were doing? I don't care about it. I want these guys. So, tell me. What are you leaving out?"

The man looked at the cop, then back at Axel. He blinked and looked down at his hands. "Earl didn't deserve to die."

"I'm sure he didn't. So, why don't you help me get Earl a little justice."

"Justice," the man repeated. Then he sighed. "They took some stuff."

"What kind of stuff?" Axel demanded.

The guy fidgeted and shook his head. He scowled out the back window of the car. "Guns," he finally muttered. "Cash."

Axel didn't allow himself to swear, though that's what he wanted to do. "And why didn't you tell him?" Axel said, jamming a finger toward the officer. "Or any other law enforcement."

"The guns aren't registered to us, and I didn't tell my father-in-law I took them. The cash?" The poacher licked his lips, and his eyes darted back and forth.

The man was not good at lying. Likely the cash was from some underhanded dealings. Ones Axel didn't have time to care about. "That all?"

The man scrunched his face up. "They made me give them my car keys. It's not parked here, but I told them where it's parked a few miles out."

"A car? They stole your car and you're just now telling us?" Axel knew his voice was a little too sharp when this man had just lost his friend, but he couldn't bring himself to care.

"Just the keys. They'd have to get to it first. I... The car is my wife's, and she's going to leave me if she finds out I got caught poaching again."

"I want the make and model of the car," Axel bit out. "License plate number. You don't know it? You're going to be breaking the bad news to your wife a lot sooner than you'd like. Then you tell me exactly where you left it."

The poacher rattled off the information, still staring at his hands. Axel noted everything down in his phone and sent a quick text message to Opaline, Rihanna and Alana. Between the three of them, the information would get out to all the necessary authorities.

The difficult part was that the men were now confirmed as armed. They'd killed together, which meant they would kill again, given the chance. Authorities had to be extra careful.

Axel had to hope no one did anything stupid before he and Selena could track them down. Axel glanced back at the cabin. Selena was still inside with Blanca. If she'd found anything, they should head out.

He gave one last look at the poacher, who appeared as miserable as possible. Axel didn't think there was any information left to get from him, so he turned to walk away. It was time to move.

"You're going to bring those SOBs in?" the man asked.

Axel stopped and glanced at the poacher over his shoulder. The shock he'd been under when Axel had first arrived had worn off and shifted into anger. Axel understood. "That's my job."

The man nodded. "Good. Well, I'd cooperate in whatever it took to get them behind bars. Earl didn't deserve to die. He wasn't perfect, but he didn't deserve to die. Not like this."

Not like this. Yeah, Axel knew that feeling all too well.

He headed for the cabin, instructing the local cop that he could take the poacher into the station. He opened the door. Selena was crouched by a rudimentary fireplace, Blanca sniffing something.

He rubbed his hands together. "A little warmer in here than out there," he offered by way of greeting.

"A little. Looks like they had a fire going. There's a glove left behind, but who knows if it belonged to the guys we're looking for." Selena pointed to the glove Blanca was sniffing.

"We know they're in the area," Axel said. "We know they were in here, and the poacher said this cabin was his friend's and they hadn't been up here in a month or so because of the snow. His buddy was shot before they entered, so I think the likelihood of it belonging to or at least used by one of the escapees is high."

"Agreed," Selena said, standing up from her crouched position.

"Stole a car, guns and cash."

Selena swore.

"My thoughts exactly. Poacher said the car was a few miles out. They took his keys. I imagine that's what they headed for."

Selena nodded, motioning for Blanca to follow her to the door.

"Why don't you drive? We'll track, make sure the glove is one of theirs. I'll keep in touch and meet you at where this car was parked."

Axel studied her. She was dead serious. And out of her mind. "Nice try."

She puffed out a breath, her distractingly full mouth curving slightly. "It was worth a shot," she offered.

"Was it?" he returned, working hard to keep his voice light and even. Close quarters with Selena Lopez was not high on his list of ways to torture himself. "You know you're not going to work alone."

"I'm not alone. I have Blanca."

Axel looked up at the dog, waiting patiently by the door. Then at her again. He raised an eyebrow.

She rolled her eyes. "Yeah, yeah. We're in pairs for this one. So, you want to drive to where the car was?"

Axel nodded. "I've gotten the information out, so hopefully someone will catch sight of them in the car."

Selena frowned. "If not, Blanca isn't going to be able to track a car. Certainly not in time to stop them from crossing the border."

Axel nodded. "They won't stay in the car long. They'll assume it'll be tagged. My guess is they find some place to stay, then get a new car. But they're going to want to stay as rural as possible to avoid detection. At some point, they might even camp."

Selena looked out the open door dubiously. "You couldn't pay me to camp in the dead of February." Her expression went thoughtful. "You know, I was thinking about that. Why plan this escape in February? Why not wait till April or May when you might have more survivable weather?"

Axel considered. He'd been focused on the poachers and hadn't thought about the time of year. Selena was right. If it was just about escape, they would have waited for a better time of year.

"So, there's more to it."

"Has to be. Don't you think?"

Axel nodded. "Come on. Let's get to the Jeep and see if we find anything where they took the car."

"Got it, boss," Selena said, stepping outside, Blanca at her heels.

"Don't call me that," he muttered, following her.

"What?" she said, grinning over her shoulder at him. "Boss?"

He didn't scowl, didn't allow himself to. He kept his expression as neutral as possible. "Yes."

"But are you not, technically, my boss?"

"I'm not—"

"Your title is *supervisory* special agent, right? That seems to imply, or perhaps even straight out say, you are something of a *supervisor*."

Axel didn't say anything to that. Though it *was* his official position title, it was more about seniority and the chain of command than wanting to place himself above anyone in the team. They had to be a *team*. Not boss-employee. As full supervisor, Alana felt the same way. It was why they were a successful FBI division. They'd worked hard to foster a community of teamwork and equality, to avoid any politicking or grandstanding to get positions over each other.

And mostly, he didn't want Selena thinking of him as her *boss*. It made his shoulders tense in a way he didn't want to analyze too deeply.

"That's what I thought," she said with a sultry chuckle. She sauntered off toward the Jeep, and Axel tried *very* hard not to watch her.

Chapter Four

Selena watched the forest pass as Axel drove to where the poacher had said his car would be. Sun glinted off the snow, glittery, white and beautiful. She wasn't sure how long they'd have the luxury of heat blasting from the vents, so she tried to soak up all that she could.

Finding the escapees in a car was going to be more difficult, especially with their head start, but she didn't mind avoiding a hike through the woods. No matter how the sun shone, the air was *cold*.

More to it. Why would three men escape prison in the midst of this? Why would that be the plan? "Do we know if they have any connections in Canada? Maybe it's not the final destination. Maybe it's stop one."

"Maybe. Maybe it was just a…chance. Happenstance. They saw a moment of weakness to escape and they used it."

Selena shook her head. "No. It was too coordinated. And the three of them… There has to be something they have in common. The briefing didn't say anything about them knowing each other on the outside."

"No. They didn't, as far as we know."

"There's a piece we're missing."

Axel nodded grimly. "I agree. But right now our job isn't the pieces, it's tracking them down."

Selena didn't say anything to that. She wasn't so sure they shouldn't be trying to figure out the puzzle. Sure, some of the people back at headquarters were doing that, and as an agent she specialized in tracking and suspect apprehension, not investigation, but that didn't mean investigating wouldn't get them closer to apprehension.

Axel slowed the car, squinting into the midmorning sun. "It's still there."

"You're sure that's the car?" She could only see a flash of silver—not enough to make out the model yet.

"Silver sedan. In the exact place he said." Axel came to a complete stop. "If it's still there, they might be too."

Selena studied their surroundings, as Axel did. She didn't see a sign of anyone, but that didn't mean they weren't out there. Waiting.

"I'll get Blanca out and we'll track using the glove. You search the car."

She waited for Axel to argue. To say they should stick together. With the potential for attack, they couldn't split up.

"Vests," was all he said.

They had their tactical gear in the rear cargo space, so when Axel slid out of the car, Selena did the same. They moved quickly and silently, watching and bracing themselves for a surprise attack.

But they met at the trunk with no hint that anyone else was near them. Axel held out her vest, and she took it. They both shed their jackets, pulled the Kevlar vests on, tightened the straps and shrugged back into their coats.

Then, in nonverbal agreement, they went completely still and silent, listening to their surroundings.

The wind whistled through the trees, and snow blew so hard it sounded like pebbles being tossed in the wind. Any slight noises made by anyone else would be lost.

There would be no way to *hear* if anyone else was around, though the wind might have also drowned out the sound of their car approaching, depending on how close the men were to the silver sedan. Maybe she and Axel would have a chance to sneak up on them.

Selena nodded toward the car, a signal she was going to let Blanca out and begin to track.

Axel nodded his head, green eyes cool and assessing. He had many sides to him. This was the man back in the car this morning who'd driven too fast to stop a murder that had already happened.

They both crouched behind the car, guns drawn and ready, and Selena knew she had to say…something to keep his focus on the task at hand, not the life they'd lost.

"We take all three in alive, they'll fold on each other. They'll go back to jail for a very long time."

His gaze met hers, green and cold. She might have shivered, but there was something about Axel. She didn't know what it was, didn't *want* to know what it was, only that it always had things shifting around in her chest. A flutter. A sense of…not just wanting. Something far more complicated than that.

The worst part was, she got the impression he felt it too. The way their gazes held just a little too long in moments like this. When they should be moving forward. Acting.

And where did you end up the last time you thought a guy felt the same thing you did?

She held his gaze out of her own warped sense of spite, but she struggled to find her equilibrium here, in the depth of green that reminded her of a spring forest rather than the winter white they were surrounded by.

"Got it," he said.

She'd forgotten what point she'd made, but she wouldn't dwell on that. She gave Blanca a quick pet, then held out the glove. Blanca sniffed. Moved ahead a few feet, came back to sniff again.

Selena kept her gun drawn, her eyes scanning the area around Blanca. Blanca did her job, sniffing and inching forward. She was struggling to find the scent. Selena knew they had to get closer to the car, but she wanted Axel to clear the area before she moved Blanca in.

"Clear," Axel called after a few minutes.

Surprised, Selena jogged over to the car.

"They were stuck," Axel said, pointing to where the tires were lodged deep in the snow and, below that, mud. "Ran the car till the gas tank was empty, probably trying to get out. Engine is still hot, but they're gone."

"If they did that, I can't imagine they're too far ahead of us."

"No, they can't be. We'll grab our packs and follow Blanca. I imagine the car should give her a good scent to go on."

Selena nodded. "You get the packs. I'll search the interior."

Axel nodded, and Selena jerked the driver's side door open. There was the smallest hint of warmth still in the interior, but it dissipated quickly as Selena leaned inside. She wanted clothing, preferably. Nothing in the front seat, but as she moved to look into the back, something on the floorboard caught her eye.

She was already wearing gloves, so she reached down and picked it up. It was a prisoner ID card.

Peter Lopez.

She looked at the face of a man she didn't know. One her father had expected her to save. How had he gotten tangled up with murderers and batterers? He'd been arrested during a drug deal that had gone wrong, but his sentence was shorter because in the trial it had been proven he hadn't been carrying a weapon.

He was still responsible for fleeing the scene of a murder, and for dealing, but if there was anything Selena had ever comforted herself with—and likely why Opaline still thought Peter could be saved, and expected Selena to *help* save him, just like Dad did—it was that he wasn't in prison for a violent crime.

Or hadn't been. Maybe he'd been the one to pull the trigger on the innocent poacher back there. Maybe this was the end of the line for Peter. And there was no doubt in her mind that Dad *and* Opaline would blame her for that.

"Selena?"

Selena didn't startle—she was too well trained—but she closed her eyes and immediately chastised herself. She'd told Alana she could handle this case without her personal feelings getting in the way, and she *had* to make certain not to make a liar out of herself.

"Prison ID left behind," she said, reaching backward to show Axel, who stood outside the car behind her. "You were right, they were definitely in the car."

Axel took the ID. "Anything Blanca can track?"

Without moving and giving away the fact she hadn't fully searched the car yet, Selena looked into the back seat out of the corner of her eye.

"Clothes in the back. But even if they sat in here, this isn't their car. Too many competing smells. Give me a few minutes to use the glove around here to see if she gets a trail scent."

Selena scooted out of the car and stood, Axel way too close for comfort. Luckily he wasn't looking at her. He was frowning into the woods.

"They got guns, a car and cash from the poacher. The car is stuck."

Selena worked with Blanca while Axel mused aloud.

"They warm up, then take off again. There has to

be a plan to get supplies. They can't make it to Canada on foot without food and water."

Selena held the car open while Blanca sniffed the back seat. "Plenty of hunting cabins and the like scattered around. Could be they expect to find shelter and food as they hike along."

Axel's frown deepened as he pulled his phone out of his pocket. "I wonder if Opaline could get us an idea of where the cabins on the route to Canada are."

"Maybe, but how would they have anything like that? As far as we know from the prison, they got clothes and the security guard's gun. That's it." Selena looked at the winter landscape around them. "Unless they had more help than that."

Axel's expression was grim. "That's what I'm afraid of."

Blanca moved forward, gave one bark, then sat and waited for further instruction. "She's got a scent. We can pack up and follow?"

Axel nodded. "I'll update the team."

Selena waited by Blanca. The dog would wait for the signal to search, though she all but vibrated sitting there in the snow. It was a good sign. She had a good scent on at least one of the fugitives, but Selena worried about the snow. It wouldn't stop Blanca from tracking, but melting snow could hinder their progress.

"I guess I have to be grateful it's so darn cold," Selena muttered.

AXEL BROUGHT THEIR packs to where Blanca waited to search. A cold, isolated landscape.

Selena was right. There were a few threads that didn't make sense, and Axel knew their priority had to be this search. But when there was a mystery, a puzzle, what he really wanted to do was sit down and sort through it.

"We've got teams of two moving in from the Canadian border," he told her. "Local police notified of the information we have. It'd take some serious planning and skill to evade capture." Or help from a bigger, stronger threat.

Selena secured her pack on. "Ready?"

Axel nodded and she gave Blanca the *search* command.

Blanca immediately moved forward. There were some footprints, but the wind had blown snow over them so they were just little indentations in the snow. Likely they'd be completely gone before they followed the dog for a mile.

They walked in silence for a while, pausing when Blanca paused, then following behind her again when she moved forward. "I'm not sure how much of a head start they've got, but she'd be moving faster or signaling if they were close. She does either of those two things, we'll want to pause and draw our weapons."

Axel nodded. He'd never worked this closely with Selena and Blanca before. While he prided himself on being a team player who didn't use the "supervisory" part of his title to take over any assignment, it was an odd sensation to be completely beholden to how Selena decided to use her dog.

Axel watched the time as they walked, routinely checked to see if there were any updates from the team and mostly tried not to think about the subzero wind chill.

"Let's take a water break," Selena suggested, and it took Axel a moment to realize she meant for the dog. "Pause."

Blanca immediately stopped. Selena shrugged off her pack and got out a water bottle and a dish. The dog eagerly lapped up the water, and Selena took her own swig. When their gazes locked, Axel didn't look away.

He should. He knew he should. They didn't need to constantly be staring at each other a little too long when there was work to be done. But he wouldn't be the one who looked away first. She was the one who'd always avoided this...*thing* between them. Not that he pressed the issue, but she'd set the precedent to ignore it.

And now was *not* the time to play these mind games with himself.

Selena looked down at her pack, dug around until she came up with a dog treat. She tossed the Milk-Bone at him, Blanca's eyes following the treat even as she stood completely still.

"She's still not sure about you," Selena said casually.

Axel frowned at Selena, then at the dog, whose focus was on the treat in his hand. "Excuse me?"

"She likes you, but she's not sure about you. Just in case you need to give her commands, you need to suck up to her a little."

"I need to suck up to your dog?"

Selena nodded. There was humor in her eyes, but her expression was serious. And Axel wasn't comfortable with the serious nature of the reasoning. "Why wouldn't you be able to give her commands?"

Selena shrugged. "We're law enforcement, Axel. Don't pretend like you don't know what could happen."

No, it was never far out of his mind, but there was something about the dog that added a weird weight to all the things that could go wrong in their profession. He shook his head and crouched, holding out the treat. "Come."

Blanca trotted over and took the treat from his fingers, then she stood in front of him and let him scratch her behind the ears. "There's a girl. I miss having a dog," he murmured, more to himself and the dog than Selena.

"You don't have one out on that farm of yours?" Selena replied, packing the supplies away. "What's the point in space if you don't have a dog?"

"I'm gone too much, so I've had to settle for animals that don't need constant care. Chickens. Cows. I was thinking about getting a goat."

She laughed. It wasn't something she did a lot around him. Sometimes he'd hear her talking to Carly, and she'd laugh like that. It hit him a little too hard out here in the snowy wilderness, just the two of them.

"A goat?" she said, somewhat disbelieving as she adjusted the pack back on her shoulders.

Axel shrugged, trying to keep a casual grin on his face. "Sure. They're good at keeping a lawn tidy."

She shook her head, her mouth curved into a smile. She seemed relaxed enough, and he'd never gotten much of that with Selena. "Search," she commanded Blanca.

They set out again, and Axel couldn't help wanting to let the moment stretch out a bit. "You know, I was reading this article about a former NHL player who raises llamas. Maybe that's what I'll do in my retirement."

He got another husky laugh out of her. "Llamas. You've lost it, Morrow. Besides. You? Retire?"

"Sure. We all have to sometime."

"I don't know. You seem like one of those guys who'd just transition into the guy in charge. Not retire and putter around at your farm."

"Lots to putter around with on a farm, no matter how old or small. It's peaceful. It's home. Sometimes I look forward to it."

"And the other times?"

"I'm glad I have a challenging job that keeps my mind occupied." Though the older he got the more he wondered if keeping his mind occupied kept him from fully dealing with things he'd have to face eventually. Or maybe he wouldn't. Maybe he'd let the loss of his family define him and keep him from ever building new, deep bonds that went beyond work friendships. It didn't seem so bad when he was working.

Only when he was home on his farm. Alone.

"Now, keeping a mind occupied I understand," Selena said, stifling a yawn. "I don't think we're going to catch up to them at this pace."

"No, but we'll stay close. And unless they've magically found supplies somewhere, we should be able to keep going longer than they do."

But that *unless* hung between them, because they both thought there might be more to it. Help somewhere. A plan TCD hadn't figured out yet.

"Tell me about Peter."

She clammed up immediately. The easy curve of her mouth gone, any light in her eyes vanishing in a second. He might have regretted focusing back on the task at hand, but the tightening in his gut wasn't at all appropriate for the situation. Better to focus on what they should, even if it made her uncomfortable.

"I've told you all there is to tell," she said, her voice as cold as the world around them.

"So, why was Opaline so upset?"

"Opaline's…emotional. I know you guys see the happy, bubbly side of her, but there's the other side of that. She feels things…deeply. It's just who she is."

"And you aren't emotional?"

"I'm an FBI agent, Axel. That's what I am."

"Last time I checked, FBI agents got to be human."

She snorted derisively. "You can say that because you're a man."

"Fair enough. The point I'm trying to make, though, is… You get to have some feelings about this. Even if once we catch up to them, you push them aside and do the job."

"Or I can handle it my way. Thanks all the same."

"It might help the case, Selena."

She whipped her head around to stare daggers at him. "I'm not sure how my father and Opaline thinking I should be able to save Peter, convince him to follow the straight and narrow, has anything to do with the case. I don't know the kid. I've been responsible for him for half my life and I don't *know* the guy. I don't know his friends. I don't know what he's capable of, and if you think Opaline might, that's a laugh and a half, because she thinks she can save anyone if she forgives and forgets. Well, I don't believe in forgiving and forgetting betrayal, and I don't believe in ignoring that people have their own free will. Peter made his choices. I don't know how or why. I only know I'll make sure he pays for them. And if that makes me a crappy person? So damn be it. Because my *job* is what I care about. It's who I am. The end."

Axel didn't say anything to that. She wouldn't listen anyway. Still, it was hardly *the end.* That was a lesson he'd had to learn the hard way, and no doubt she was in the midst of learning it.

She wouldn't appreciate his understanding, so he kept it to himself. Just like attraction. His own doubts and conflicting emotions about the assignment. *Keep it to yourself. Bury it down deep.*

And hope the dam that kept it all inside never broke.

Chapter Five

Selena didn't mind losing her temper when the situation called for it, but this was not that situation. She'd been…hurt. God, she was an idiot. But they'd been talking. She'd actually been enjoying his company without being too worried about the whole attraction thing.

Then he'd asked her about Peter. Like sharing genetic material made him *her* responsibility.

Why did everyone in her life want to make Peter her responsibility?

She blew out a breath slowly, willing her anger to cool, her heartbeat to calm. She'd spewed all that at Axel, and that had been a mistake. She knew this was going to be an assignment fraught with them. She would deal with that by promising herself those mistakes would only be here, in these quiet moments.

When they had to act, really act, all of this conflicting, ancient history garbage would be shoved aside to do her job. If she lost her temper in the *waiting* that was so much of her job, well, she'd forgive herself. She *was* human.

So was he.

"I don't know him," Selena said calmly. "I don't have some secret understanding of who he is as a person, who he might be connected to. Fair or not, everyone in my life has expected me to in a variety of ways. I'm not here because Peter Lopez is my estranged half brother. I'm here because Blanca and I make a good team apprehending suspects. I need you to understand that."

Axel was quiet as they walked. When he finally spoke, she got the feeling he'd really *thought* about what she'd said. "Understood," he offered.

She thought he might…actually do just that. An odd feeling when she'd felt misunderstood and maligned for a really, *really* long time. First with her family and their insistent need for her to be the one who handled *everything*, and then at her last department when…

Well, it didn't do to dwell on all the ways she'd been humiliated and embarrassed. She snuck a glance at Axel. Maybe it was good to remember that sleeping with a coworker, especially in law enforcement, never ended well for the woman.

Blanca paused, scenting the air, her body vibrating in a way that spoke to an excitement. Either they were close, or the scent trail was clear enough she wanted to take off. But Selena had a feeling they were quickly catching up to the escapees.

Who were armed and dangerous.

Selena held up her hand and drew her weapon. Axel did the same. Instinctually, they moved so they were almost back to back, protecting themselves from being surprised. A unit that could see in both directions.

"Close?" Axel asked quietly.

"Within shooting distance," Selena murmured, eyeing the trees around them. Blanca's positioning meant the three men were not all in one direction. Were they fanning out to surround them?

"We're easy pickings right here. We need cover," Axel said. "See anything?"

Selena scanned the area in front of her. "Some dead trees. We'll have to lie in the snow, but they'd give us some cover." Not enough. Not from all sides. But that was the risk of the job.

"You go first. Then call Blanca. Then I'll follow."

"Got it." Selena moved slowly and carefully, on full alert. She studied the pile of logs, tried to adjust and rearrange them in her mind to give themselves the best tactical advantage. They'd still have to lie in the snow, and dead trees weren't exactly bulletproof shields, but it was something. She crouched and said softly and forcefully, "Blanca. Come."

There was a moment of hesitation from the dog—she wanted to do her job, track—but she obeyed Selena's command. Selena pointed to the spot she wanted Blanca— behind both the tree cover and Selena herself. If they had anyone sneak up from behind, Blanca would sound the alarm.

"Clear," Selena said to Axel.

He started moving toward her, and almost immediately a shot rang through the quiet air. Selena flinched, and Axel dived to the ground. Selena felt her heart leap to her throat.

"Hit?" she called out, hoping her voice didn't sound as panicked as she'd felt.

"No," Axel replied through gritted teeth. He was army crawling through the thick snow, which couldn't be comfortable.

Selena couldn't see anything. Wherever they were was either too far away or too well camouflaged. Another shot rang out. She ducked. When she peeked her head over the dead tree, Axel still had his head in the snow.

"Morrow," she barked.

He shook his head and started crawling again. Each inch seemed to take forever, and she had to fight back the need to jump out and pull him into the makeshift cover.

He was fine. Not shot. Just trying to avoid it. He was a skilled agent. They might be a team, but it wasn't her job to *protect* him, just to have his back. The fact that *protect* seemed to be an instinctual need inside her was perplexing.

Luckily, she didn't have time to think about it. After what felt like hours and was maybe minutes, Axel crawled over the logs and laid himself next to her. He faced the same direction she did.

"Two shooters in front of us," he said, his voice low but not a whisper. Too deep and authoritative to be called a whisper. "If there's a third, he hasn't fired yet."

"How do you know it's two shooters?"

"Sound of the gun. Angle of the shot." Axel lifted his own gun and rested it on the log in front of him.

"What about the third? Coming from behind?"

Axel glanced over his shoulder. "Blanca will warn us, don't you think?"

"I know. She'll bark, once, the minute anyone's within forty feet of us."

"Good. So, they're still a ways off."

Another shot rang out, and they both ducked again. Selena couldn't tell where the shots were hitting.

"Bad aim?" she asked.

Axel shook his head. "They're just too far away to get a good shot. They're trying to keep us far away, though. Don't get me wrong, they get the chance, they'll kill us, but right now these are warning shots."

"Why not come and kill us?"

Axel was quiet for a moment, clearly considering. "I suppose the risk they'd get shot in the process. They're more worried about escape than adding more crimes to their rap sheet?"

"Escaping prison isn't going to do them any favors. And they already added another murder to their rap sheet. Axel, there has to be something more they're trying to do than escape. I can't imagine all this is just to be free."

"Men have done far less just to be free."

But it didn't set right. These were career criminals. Her brother had been in trouble with the law since he'd turned thirteen. A prison sentence was hardly unexpected. It was a risk he was well aware of—a path he'd chosen to go down knowing full well what the consequences might be.

Another shot, but Axel and Selena had their heads below the logs so there was no ducking this time.

"They're retreating," Axel noted.

"How can you tell?"

"Sound of the gun. The direction they're coming from isn't so spread out. They'll keep shooting, even out of range, in the hopes the sound of the gunfire will keep us off their tails. Only two are shooting—which leads me to believe one is doing everything he can to hide their tracks."

"They can't hide from Blanca's nose."

Axel nodded.

"We shouldn't fall for it. We've got vests and we're trained FBI agents. Sitting here being scared of a little gunfire doesn't complete the mission."

"They're heading right toward the rest of our team. All we have to do is keep behind them like this, make sure they don't slip through any cracks. Eventually we'll have a tight enough circle to bring them in without a dangerous shootout."

Selena didn't particularly care for the slow, patient approach. It meant more days out in the wilderness alone with Axel. But she knew his plan was one that would be best to safeguard the team.

Trying not to scowl, Selena settled into the cold snow around her. "How long?"

"Until we don't hear the gunshots any longer."

IT TOOK FAR too long. Axel was doing everything to keep his teeth from chattering. Even in layers of tactical gear, lying in the snow was cold, uncomfortable business. Once they'd gone a good ten minutes without hearing a gunshot, Axel motioned for Selena to sit up.

"How's Blanca in this cold?" he asked. The dog had remained alert and still the entire time.

"She'll need a break eventually, but she's good for a few more hours yet."

"Good. I think we're safe to get up out of the snow now, but let's call in."

"And give them more of a head start? Let's get going and call on the way."

She was too impatient. It wasn't her usual MO, so Axel had to wonder what was driving it. The cold? Her brother's connection? The same things that bothered him about being out in the expansive wilderness with only her and her dog?

Best not to think too much on it. Focus on what needed to be done. What he'd really like to do was find somewhere warm to change into dry clothes, but that wasn't an option.

He settled himself on the log, Selena beside him. Blanca would warn them if the escapee trio doubled back. Axel pulled out his phone and started a conference call with Aria and Max.

They popped on, seated next to their respective partners. Both screens showed two people, perfectly warm and indoors.

"I hate you all right now," Selena said grimly.

Aria grinned from the screen. "Got a nice fire going. Some hot chocolate ready for marshmallows. It's actually so warm I might have to take off my sweater. What do you think, Carly?"

Selena snorted in disgust as Carly smiled ruefully next to Aria on the screen.

"You're going to have to move out of the cozy digs," Axel offered, not above a little jealousy himself. "We want a tighter circle."

"Something happen?" Max asked.

"We got too close, and they took a few shots," Selena said with a shrug. "Too far away to do any damage."

Carly frowned, and Aria's humorous expression got very serious.

"Do you have the map of cabins in the area Opaline sent?" Axel asked.

They all had the partner not holding the phone pull up the maps on their phones.

"Right now we've got a triangle of sorts, with our trio right in the middle," Axel confirmed. "We need to make our triangle smaller, keeping them in the middle. They're armed and they're going to shoot, so we want to be slow, steady and careful."

"There has to be something more to this," Selena said, hugging her arms around herself. "It's miserable out here. No one *plans* to escape prison in the middle of February unless they've got to accomplish something in the here and now. In whatever downtime you guys have, see what you can come up with."

"But first, we want everyone moving in closer," Axel said.

Selena tapped the interactive map on her phone as Axel looked over at her screen. There were three cabins they could use to try and surround the fugitives.

"Axel and I will move to the one I've marked three." Selena said, glancing at him for agreement.

He gave a nod.

"Aria and Carly, you'll take cabin two. Max and Scott, you'll base at one. Our escapees are currently closest to three, but heading toward one and two. As Axel and I head for three, we'll be following them toward one and two. Think of your cabins as bases. You'll want to take turns patrolling the area in between. We've got Blanca, which means we'll be able to stop any backtracks. Our main concern is them taking a longer route to the east or west rather than the straight shot toward the border."

"We'll call Rihanna and see if there are some local law enforcement who we could get stationed in the east and west," Max said, all business. "Small departments in these parts, if any, but maybe we can get a county to lend some manpower beyond the APB."

"Good idea," Axel agreed. "I think they'll take the straight shot, but we can't be too careful. Armed. Dangerous. I want everyone to understand that. Leonard Koch has already killed someone. Cold-blooded. We have to assume anyone associating with him has the same capability. We want these guys, but we want to be smart and safe."

"They can't do much damage in the middle of no-where, upper Michigan, can they?" Aria offered. "I haven't seen a soul around this cabin."

"One man is already dead," Axel replied flatly, try-ing not to sound too much like a superior dressing down a subordinate. Aria was a rookie, but she was good at her job. Still, lives had already been lost, and they all needed to remember that. "A man who had nothing to do with any of this. Keep that in mind."

They all nodded their assent, then closed the call. Axel could *feel* Selena's steady gaze on him. He didn't look toward it. He put his phone away.

"Will it bother you forever?" she asked quietly.

Axel frowned, turning to glance at her. "What?"

"That a man died. A man you didn't know, that you had no responsibility to. It bothers you now. I'm just curious if that sticks with you forever." She was too close, her dark eyes too discerning.

Axel wasn't sure he was comfortable with the ques-tion, and he definitely wasn't comfortable with the answer. Especially when she kept talking, right here sitting hip to hip on the log.

"Innocent people have died during assignments I've been on," she said, her gaze never leaving his. "I've never felt responsible. They don't haunt me. So, I'm just wondering if I'm cold-blooded, or if you get over it."

"You're not cold-blooded," Axel muttered.

"How do you know?"

"You care about your brother, that much is clear." Her expression shuttered, and she looked away. Which, yeah, he'd been going for. "You care about Opaline. You hide it all, compartmentalize it all, but you've got family issues up to the hilt, Selena, and you wouldn't if you didn't care. If you were cold."

She stood abruptly, adjusting her pack and ignoring him completely.

He blew out a breath. He should let it go at that. Keep his mouth shut. But she'd asked him a question, and he felt some...*need* to answer her. To try to make her understand what he felt.

"It's not the individual deaths that haunt me. It's the feeling of being too late. When you lose your family the way I did, when you survive, you start to realize that timing is everything. And it's the one thing beyond your control. You can be the best damn FBI agent out there, and you might still be two seconds too late."

"So why be an FBI agent at all, knowing that you'll be faced with the uncontrollable timing part of things?"

"Because if you never face the things that haunt you, Selena, they eat you alive."

She stared down at him a moment, something that looked a lot like shell shock in her expression. She frowned, shook it away and then held out a gloved hand.

It was an offer of teamwork. Help him up off the log though he didn't need it. But it put them back on equal, mission footing.

Or it was supposed to. Even though they both wore gloves, fitting his hand into hers, letting her help pull him to his feet, it ignited a dangerous warmth that spread through him. He should have immediately let her hand go once on his feet, but he didn't.

He held on, stood far too close and looked down at her face. Dark eyes, cheeks and nose pink with cold. She was a complicated woman with a complicated past, and they were on a *very* complicated mission. Everything was dangerous and required a delicate balance.

But here they were, in this side moment, separate from everything else. Touching hands. Looking at each other, and he thought, most dangerous of all, *understanding* each other.

She didn't pull away. He didn't let her go. They didn't speak, and they didn't move. They simply looked at each other, breathing in time with one another. He could imagine what it would be like if he did. If he stepped closer, if he pulled her to him, if he fitted his mouth to hers.

It was like a mirage in front of him, one he wanted to lean into.

Her phone buzzed in her pocket, breaking the moment.

Thank God.

Chapter Six

It took a moment for the buzzing to break through the odd static in Selena's brain. A static she didn't understand. She'd been made stupid by lust and inexperience once. This was neither. It was something far…bigger.

Far scarier.

But the phone buzzed incessantly in her pocket, and she finally thought to drop Axel's hand and dig out her device. It was her sister calling.

There were so many reasons she didn't want to deal with Opaline right now, but it very well could be about the task at hand. The task at hand being searching for and apprehending criminals, *not* having weird out-of-body experiences with Axel.

And, wow, what would an in-*body experience with Axel feel like?*

"Hello," she greeted too harshly, trying to get the image of *anything* with Axel out of her mind.

"Selena. You were shot at?" Opaline demanded. Her voice reminded Selena of their childhood. Opaline was older. She'd taken that role seriously, but something about their parents' divorce had seemed to flip their roles. Opaline had turned emotional and needy and at sea. She'd thrown herself at people, men in particular, always looking for safety. For shore. Selena had to take over being the one who could handle anything and everything their mother and father threw at them.

Selena had gotten away from that as soon as she'd been able.

But this sounded like concern, with a hint of scolding, which was far more big sistery than Opaline had acted in over a decade. It made Selena's heart twist uncomfortably with a hope she thought she'd eradicated a long time ago.

"Shot at is probably an exaggeration. There was shooting, but it was far away." She couldn't help but try to soothe. After Dad had ruined everything, Selena had been the one to pick up the pieces. But maybe they were adult enough now that they could find a way to bridge the gaps in their relationship.

"Do you think Peter was the one shooting?" Opaline asked in a hushed whisper.

The bubble of hope burst in an instant. It was always that. Always about Peter. Never about her. Why did that still hurt? She'd kept herself separate and away, and still Opaline could cut her in two. Over their *half* brother. "I don't know," Selena said flatly.

"I hate that you're out there as enemies."

"His choice, Opaline. Did you call about something in particular?"

"He's our brother."

"I'm your sister."

There was a silence, charged with hurt. But how was that fair? "You don't need my help, my support. You never did," Opaline said softly—the opposite of her usual loud demeanor. "But Peter did."

Selena didn't know what to do with that, even less so when she could practically *feel* Axel watching her, listening to her side of the conversation. Picking it apart. No doubt thinking of all the ways she should be responsible for Peter.

"You gave up on him," Opaline said, sounding more like herself. Overemotional. Laying the blame on Selena's blameless shoulders.

Or does she just sound like Mom?

Selena was in the middle of an important assignment. She couldn't cry. She couldn't indulge in self-pity. She had to set this aside and move on. Ignoring all the feelings it churned up. "I'm sorry you feel that way," Selena said robotically. It was how she talked to her mother too. "Maybe at some point you'll understand that while you were all so busy trying to save Peter, some of us needed help and support too." She tried to hold her tongue, ice out the emotions, but those words…

You gave up on him.

It hurt because it was true. She had given up on Peter. She didn't know how to keep believing in someone so dedicated to ruining their own life.

And when she'd needed her sister, when everything had blown up at her last job, Opaline had been so obsessed with Peter's trial and him going to jail, she hadn't bothered to ask Selena if she was all right. If *she* needed anything. Peter was her project. Selena was on her own.

They both were still on the line, in a weighted silence neither knew how to fill. Maybe Selena should just accept they never would.

"You never let me help," Opaline said, hushed and pained.

"When did you ever try?"

"When did you ever ask for any?"

Selena didn't know what to say to that. She was sure she'd asked, or at least hinted… Hadn't it been obvious to anyone after Tom had ruined her reputation that she needed someone to hold her hand—just for a little while? Someone who understood what it was like to feel betrayed by someone you'd loved, or thought you had.

"I have important work to do," Selena said. Her voice was so cold it matched the air around her. "And so do you."

"The difference, Selena, is I can care about both." The call ended with a click and echoing silence.

Why did she always handle things so badly when it came to Opaline? If she'd kept her feelings out of it—a lesson she'd been trying to impart to Opaline since their parents had started the divorce process—everything would be okay.

A lesson life had reinforced, over and over again. *So why are you still struggling?*

It was just Peter. Opaline. The perfect storm of

things she didn't want to deal with. In a few more days, after they tracked him down and Peter was in jail, Selena could leave all this *feeling* behind.

Because if you never face the things that haunt you, Selena, they eat you alive.

Axel's past was a lot more haunted than hers, so she should ignore that he'd said that. That it had clamored around inside her like church bells, too close, too loud. *Too right.*

"Everything okay?" Axel asked gently.

"Just fine." Certainly none of his business.

"It's not unnoticeable, you know," Axel said softly, almost sympathetically. But she didn't want his softness or sympathy.

"What?"

"The tension between you two."

Which was the worst thing he could have said to her. She worked so hard not to let those feelings show. The cracks in her armor. She knew the people they worked with could tell they weren't close, but to have him stand there and say it was obvious...

She would have preferred a slap to the face.

"Yeah, I'm pretty well aware," she returned, wincing at the acidic note in her own voice. Which only made her angrier. At him. At Opaline. At Peter. But mostly just herself. "And Aria made sure to let me know the tension between *us* isn't exactly unnoticeable."

AXEL COULD ADMIT that she'd shocked him into silence. It wasn't the information that surprised him—Max, on occasion, had asked what on earth was up with them. Axel had always played it off, but he knew people... sensed it. Much like sensing issues between Selena and Opaline.

But for a good four years there'd been a tacit, silent agreement between him and Selena that they would not speak of that tension. If they ignored it, it wouldn't go away, but, well, they could avoid it.

Now she'd laid it out between them. He wasn't *opposed* to that exactly. Clearly ignoring it hadn't done them any favors. But the timing was less than ideal.

"We should move out."

She laughed. Bitterly. Though he got the sense her bitterness wasn't just aimed at him, but at everything. Hard to blame her.

They got their stuff together. Selena ordered Blanca to search, and they started moving forward again, following the trail of the escapees while keeping an eye on the map and the cabin they'd try to reach by nightfall.

It was a cold, quiet and mostly miserable hike. Occasionally Blanca would pause and they'd wait, weapons drawn, ready for the next round of gunfire.

Axel began to dwell on that, to turn it over. His job right now was apprehension, but the puzzle pieces were irritating. "Why not stay and take us out?" he wondered aloud after they'd started again after another stop that yielded no gunfire.

"Oh, lots of reasons, I suppose," Selena said. All the emotions she'd had before and during Opaline's call were now wrapped up and hidden under the veneer of professional detachment. "If they kill us, there will be a bigger task force working to stop them. They might now know our numbers and don't want to risk the chance."

"Bottom line, it's clear their goal isn't just escaping to escape. It's bigger than that. Wouldn't you say?"

"I'd leave the profiling up to you," Selena replied. "That's your expertise."

It was, and Axel felt like he had a good picture of the men as individuals. It was the combination of the three men that didn't make any sense to him. Leonard Koch was a cold-blooded killer. Steve Jenson not quite as clever, but just as interested in violence. Motivated by it, in fact. Peter Lopez…he was the loose thread. The one that didn't tie in.

He glanced at Selena. Her gaze was on Blanca. They'd stopped to water the dog a few times, but Axel knew Selena wanted to get them to some shelter so the dog could rest in some warmth.

She didn't know Peter. Axel had to believe she wasn't holding anything back on that front. She cared too much about her job to thwart it. Alana had questioned Opaline herself after he and Selena had left, but the answers she'd passed along to Axel didn't help him any.

"Your brother was the getaway car driver in a murder."

"You could call him the escapee, the perp, the criminal, the suspect, et cetera, et cetera."

"Noted."

"So, he's weak. The weak link you pressure into doing something stupid."

"But what would they need him for? What does he bring to the trio?" Axel continued. Alana had sent the police report from the security guard who'd let them go, and Axel had reviewed it. Once they got to the cabin, he'd need to go over it again. Or even request new questioning for the security guard.

"It's the bigger thing we're missing. Career criminals don't escape from jail in the dead of winter unless something better is waiting for them," Selena said. "A sure deal. But there's no evidence the three men were connected in any way. They all were involved in different groups."

Axel glanced at the map, noticing how low the sun was in the sky. They should be getting close to the cabin. They were equipped to continue to hike through the night, but they'd need a rest for Blanca and a meal for him and Selena. He wanted to get to that base before true night descended.

"So, we need to look beyond the groups." But where? The problem with being on the tracking trail was he couldn't study the evidence the way he'd like.

"What about the victims?" Selena offered. "Maybe the victims of the crimes they committed connect in some way? Remember that case we had two years ago? The trafficking case that looked so similar, but we didn't find the thread until you connected the two missing people."

Axel nodded thoughtfully. "Once we get to the cabin, we'll talk to Alana. It's a good thread to pull."

"We should be getting close."

Axel nodded. They kept walking. Axel tried to work through all the angles of the case that he knew. Leonard had murdered someone. Steve had been part of a group of thugs who'd beaten another man to death. Peter had been the driver in fleeing a murder scene. They were different crimes, but all involved a dead person one way or another.

Would the three dead people connect?

Blanca stopped, barked twice.

Selena frowned. "That's not one of our signals."

Which was when Axel's nose began to burn. "Do you smell that?" he murmured. The world was dusky, the sun setting somewhere behind the trees. The faint hint of...

"Smoke," Selena said. "Surely they didn't start a fire knowing they've got a trail."

"Maybe they're trying to draw us out."

Selena crouched next to Blanca, running her hands over the dog's furry coat. She murmured encouraging words to the dog, scanning the trees herself. "What do you think, Axel?"

He really didn't know what to think. "How's Blanca holding up?"

"She'll keep going if we need to."

Axel considered that. In the dark, they could sneak up on the trio if they really were just...sitting around a fire. But he couldn't ignore the possibility it was a trap. The men had shot at them—they knew they were being tailed.

"Why doesn't any of this add up?" Axel muttered. He frowned at the eastern horizon. Something flickered. "Do you see that?"

Selena looked to where he pointed. "That's no campfire."

No, it wasn't. So what was the fire? A diversion? An attempt to hurt them? Something else altogether?

"Blanca, follow," Selena commanded her dog. When Axel fell into step next to her, she spoke quietly and started moving toward the fire, weapon drawn. Same as him.

"I think we should see what's going on. If she follows rather than leads, she'll alert us to any ambush from behind."

Axel nodded, and they crept forward. The smoke in the air got thicker and thicker, the flickering light in the distance bigger and bigger. Until they both stopped in their tracks.

A cabin was ablaze. The cabin on their map that they'd been hoping to find for a rest.

"Why on earth would they do that?" Selena asked.

But Axel didn't have an answer for her.

Chapter Seven

Selena lifted her sleeve over her mouth. The air was choked with smoke. They hadn't just set fire to the cabin. They had to have used something for it to be completely engulfed in flame like this.

"I'll get Max on the phone."

Selena nodded. Max was their explosives expert. He'd have a better idea what could have caused the fire. She didn't know what he'd be able to tell them over the phone, or if it mattered, but it was a reasonable next step. At some point the information they gathered had to lead them to some answers.

"We've got a situation," Axel said into his phone. "The cabin we were headed for is on fire. Not just a little fire. It's completely engulfed in flames."

Selena stared at the blaze, frowning as she thought back over the past few minutes. "We didn't hear anything. Everything has been quiet," Selena said more to herself than to Axel, since he was on the phone.

But he turned to face her. "You're right," he said, then relayed the information to Max on the line.

Axel held the phone to his ear so Selena couldn't hear Max's reply. While Axel conferred with Max on the phone, Selena studied the flames. They were on every side of the cabin. The chilly wind seemed to feed the blaze, and even with the snow Selena didn't foresee the fire going out any time soon.

What on earth could be the point of this?

"Max says if we didn't hear anything, explosives are unlikely," Axel said, sliding his phone back into his pocket. "The advanced blaze could have more to do with the use of accelerant, but he'd have to discuss it with someone with more expertise in fire over explosives."

"What's the point?" Selena said. "This doesn't stop us following them. In fact, it slows them down. It had to have taken time. We can't be that far behind now. We could catch them and—"

"And they could shoot us both dead. We have to be more careful than that."

Selena knew he was right, but it tested her patience. Though, that's why they did this kind of thing in pairs. To balance each other out. To work through the problems with a plan. She was trained specifically in search and apprehension, and she was very well aware of the necessary role of caution.

But I want this over.

She took a moment to breathe—though she couldn't allow herself a deep inhalation when there was so much smoke in the air. Still, she needed to remember her calm, remember her center. Her job over feelings. Her assignment over herself.

"Why did they burn it down, Axel? We can keep following them, we can even apprehend them, but there's something to that. They did it for a reason, and I think it's important we figure out what it is."

Axel studied the burning cabin grimly. "You're right."

"That's two 'you're rights' in under twenty. Should I be concerned?"

He gave her a sardonic smile, which produced an unnecessary and untimely flutter in her chest. She looked back at the blaze. "What about the owners of the cabin? Could they have a connection?"

"Opaline is on it."

She could feel his considering glance at that. She refused to fall for the bait. She kept her expression neutral. Because her sister was part of the assignment too, and she would do the work she needed to do while Selena did the work she needed to do. "Good. Now, what are we going to do about shelter? It's nearly dark."

"Wasn't there another cabin in the vicinity?"

Selena pulled out her phone and brought the map onto the screen. "Not confirmed as a cabin. A structure of some kind. No known owner."

"Some shelter is better than none, yeah?"

"Agreed. But let's follow our crew a bit beyond the fire. Make sure we've still got an idea of what direction they're heading in."

Axel nodded and shrugged off his pack. He pulled

out a headlamp. Selena wrinkled her nose. "Those look ridiculous."

Axel chuckled. "It's dark, we're tracking three escapees and you're worried about your appearance?"

She didn't snap at him about not understanding. She preferred people think her vain when she talked about appearances rather than have to explain that being a woman meant things were different. You had to look the part too. If someone *knew* you were trying to look authoritative, it undercut the effect.

So she said nothing and pulled a flashlight out of her own pack. Even in the dark she didn't miss his eye roll.

That was fine. Let him. She knew what she was about.

"Blanca. Search."

It took longer than before because the odors of the fire interfered with Blanca's sense of smell. Selena had to get out the glove and use it a few more times to ground Blanca in the search.

"Could they have set the fire to interfere with the dog?" Axel wondered aloud.

"A lot of work to go through for one search dog." They moved away from the fire, getting Blanca back into clearer air. Another sniff of the glove and she was moving at a better pace again.

Axel kept an eye on the map on his phone, determining if they were getting closer to their potential shelter or farther away.

Selena let out a sigh when Blanca lost the scent again. "It's too much. She needs a break."

"We could use one too," Axel said, clearly holding no blame for the dog, which soothed Selena some. "We'll head for the shelter. Food and rest for everyone. Our counterparts up north will keep the escapees from crossing the border. They'll likely have to stop too. They can't keep going on forever without food supplies."

But Selena wasn't convinced they didn't have access to *something*. They'd ventured out into the bleak winter. They'd burned down a building. Both things required supplies or the promise of supplies.

So many things didn't add up.

Still, they marched on through the dark and the cold and the snow. Axel navigated with his phone until they found the structure Opaline had dug up on some far-flung map.

Selena and Axel stopped in their tracks, his headlamp and her flashlight illuminating the…teeny, tiny shack. It'd be a tight squeeze for the three of them, and even with the close quarters, the gaps in the wood wouldn't give them much shelter. There was a roof with a crooked chimney, and if their shafts of light weren't creating an illusion, there appeared to be a foundation, which meant flooring without snow.

"It's better than nothing?" But Axel's voice was hardly one of certainty or relief.

"We might want to make sure there aren't bodies in there."

Axel snorted. "Allow me."

He moved forward. He didn't draw his weapon, but

he kept his hand on the butt of it in its holster. He toed the door open with his foot. It creaked and groaned like it might fall off its rusty hinges at any moment.

He swept his beam of light inside, taking his time to examine the opening. So much time Selena eventually moved forward, pointing her own flashlight inside the doorway above Axel's shoulder.

There was a small, ancient stove in the corner of the rectangle of a building, connected to that crooked chimney she'd noticed on the roof. The floor was concrete and cracked, bits of ice and snow here and there, but that could be brushed off.

If anything it had maybe been some sort of rustic hunting shelter. For one. Not two and a dog.

But the stove was a potential for warmth. "Think that thing works?"

"Only one way to find out."

They both ducked into the shack. Axel went about examining the stove while Selena pulled some of Blanca's supplies out of her pack. A blanket that would be more comfortable to lie on than the icy, cracked concrete floor.

There wasn't much room to maneuver. Occasionally they bumped hips or elbows, and Selena focused on Blanca, ignoring that the person she kept jostling into was a very large, very attractive man, and eventually got the dog situated. She was curled up in the far corner, resting on the blanket Selena had brought. She'd drunk some water, eaten some kibble and now rested her head on her paws and watched the fire be slowly brought to life by Axel.

Selena didn't have much of a choice of what to watch, but she just knew it couldn't be Axel stoking a fire. She settled herself on the cold ground next to Blanca and distracted herself with getting the food out of her pack, a water bottle, arranging it all in her lap. By the time she'd arranged and rearranged and driven herself slowly insane, Axel had the fire glowing in the stove.

She could feel its warmth on her face, though her body remained cold. She had to focus very hard not to shiver or let her teeth chatter since Axel looked perfectly comfortable.

The jerk.

He settled himself into a seated position as far away from her as he could manage. It still meant she could reach out and touch him, but at least she knew better than to do that.

He got his own food supplies out of his pack and began to eat. Selena tried to focus on the fire, but her gaze kept drifting to Axel.

"We shouldn't stay here too long," she offered. Not because she couldn't handle it, but because the escapees were moving forward.

"No. How long do you think Blanca needs?"

Selena looked at her dog resting next to her. "An hour. Maybe two."

Axel nodded, the flickering light of the fire giving his chiseled features a dangerous cast. Silly to let that flutter through her stomach. She knew better than to be attracted to danger.

"While Blanca rests, we can check in with various members of the team and do some of our own research about the victims, or what might connect these three and so on."

"Sounds good," Selena said. "What kind of research are we going to do from here, though?"

He turned his gaze to her, and she had to fight the tide of embarrassment from the knowledge that she'd been staring at him, not the fire.

"I know Peter is a sore spot."

Embarrassment gone, Selena turned her expression to stone. "Not sore," she replied. "Complicated."

"Use whatever words you like, but no matter how little interaction you've had with him, you know his past. You know what's shaped him, even if you don't know how. The other two men, I've only got rap sheets on. With Peter, I have a connection with you and Opaline, who know his whole background."

"Get to the point, Morrow."

"I want to know about Peter. Maybe if I do, I can make some connection to how he'd get wrapped up with these two much more violent characters. Their rap sheets don't add up. *They* don't add up. But maybe if I get a better picture of Peter, something will."

Selena stared at the flickering flame through the slats in the stove. What she knew about Peter wasn't much, but she believed Axel was right. As a gifted profiler, the more information he had, the more he could paint a picture and develop theories. Theories that could lead them to the answers they needed.

She just…didn't want to go here. Didn't want to remember, rehash or share.

But it was her job. So she'd just have to suck it up.

TESTING THE WATERS, and what Axel knew of Selena, he shrugged. "I can ask Opaline if you'd prefer."

Her jaw tightened. "What kind of things do you want to know?"

He bit back a smile. She couldn't always be maneuvered, but when she could it was a little too satisfying. "Everything. Just start from the beginning."

She clasped her gloved hands together, then rested one of them on the dog next to her. "We didn't find out about Peter until he was about two. His mom brought him to our mother to drop the bomb about their existence. I don't think Peter would remember that. He was a little thing."

Her expression was bland, but there was a hint at some emotion in her voice.

"Where was your father for that?"

She shrugged. "Work, I think. I don't remember the whole thing. Opaline and I walked in from school and Mom and this woman were yelling at each other and crying, and there was this little boy between them. He wasn't crying."

"So, he was used to emotional outbursts at that age?"

"I suppose. I don't know."

"How old were you?"

"Ten. Opaline was twelve."

Axel knew what it was like to have your life pulled

out from under you at a young age. Sure, death was a little more traumatizing, especially when you'd been a witness to it, but trauma was trauma, no matter the severity.

"After Mom divorced Dad, Peter and his mother lived with my dad for a while." She paused, picking at a thread on her coat. She took a deep breath. "Sometimes Dad would show up and take us to his house. Mom would tell him he couldn't. Dad would insist we had to. It was ugly, and the only reason I'm telling you that is because when we'd then go over to Dad and Mariane's, we were always…upset. Then Mariane would get upset."

"And Peter?"

"I never remember him crying. I never remember him doing much of anything except watching us." Her hand curled into a fist and then released. "I wasn't very nice to him."

"How so?"

Selena shrugged jerkily. "Opaline always played with him, read him stories. I kept my distance. Rebuffed him if he tried to play with me. At that age, I didn't understand he wasn't to blame for what my father had done. I'd only known Peter had showed up, and my life had changed irrevocably."

"You were young." Too much for a young girl to try to sort through.

"Yeah, I was. It went on like that for years. When Peter was about eight, Mariane was diagnosed with cancer. Dad got clean—I didn't realize until that point he'd been an alcoholic. Maybe drugs too. I didn't really get it until he stopped."

"Mariane died, right?"

Selena nodded. "When Peter was ten. I was in the police academy at that point. Dad did okay for a while, but I'd say by the time Peter was thirteen, Dad was drinking again. Peter was getting into trouble. Opaline was married to her first mistake in a line of many. I was working on the road, taking classes for K-9 handling, and once Dad started drinking again, I cut him off. Which cut Peter off too."

"You feel guilty." It surprised him. She'd imparted how much they weren't connected, and he'd believed they really had been separate, but there was a heavy, sad guilt in her voice that couldn't be ignored.

"He had his mother's family. He preferred them. When Dad begged that I help Peter, I tried a few times. Peter rebuffed me at every turn. I did what I could. He wouldn't have it. That's Peter. That's the thing you need to know."

But there was guilt there, whether it was warranted or not. Still, Peter was his target, not her. So, he should focus more on the information she'd given him. A few extra details to what he'd already known about the criminal.

"How was his relationship with your father?"

Selena's expression was grim. "Volatile."

"Violent?"

She took a moment, eyebrows drawing together as if she was deep in thought. "I guess not. A lot of yell-

ing. Throwing things. But they never got into a fist-
fight or anything like that. At least, not that I ever saw
or heard about."

"That's the part that's stumping me. There's nothing violent in Peter's record. Everything he's been in
for has been mostly aiding and abetting."

"And don't forget, selling drugs."

"Sure, but Leonard and Steve have a violent bent.
Where does Peter fit in?"

"We need to know who owned that cabin. There has
to be a clue in there."

She was right. Still, Axel brought up the file on Peter
he had on his phone. "Gangs. Peter was involved in a
lot of gang stuff. So was Steve. But not Leonard Koch."

Selena's expression went thoughtful. She looked…
gentler in the firelight. Softer. He was under no illu-
sions she was either, but he had to wonder if there was
this side to her, just hidden deep down under the professional, put-together facade she seemed to need.

"No ties to gangs at all?" she asked.

"No. Leonard Koch's misdeeds were almost always
done on his own. He's not a man who works with a
team, but he has one now."

Selena tapped her own phone, frowning over something. "The security guard's statement, did you read
it?"

"Yeah. She says Leonard was the ringleader in the
escape, in threatening her."

Selena tapped her fingers on her knee and Axel

brought up his Leonard Koch profile while snacking on the nuts he'd pulled out of his pack.

"There is one arrest on Leonard's record where he wasn't working alone, but the charges were dropped," Axel said as he skimmed the information.

"Who was he working with?" Selena asked.

Axel kept reading. "A man named Bernard McNally."

Selena tapped a few keys on her phone. "Bernard McNally." She let out a low whistle. "Well, he's clean as far as I can tell. Nothing since that incident."

Axel was already typing a text to Opaline and Alana. "We'll get a full background check from headquarters on him. See if something adds up. Connects." He grinned over at her. "See, a little rest did us good."

She grunted. "We'll see."

Chapter Eight

Selena dreaded leaving the shelter they'd found. It was uncomfortable, she was way too close to Axel Morrow and the subtle smell of his soap or cologne or something male and a little too enticing, but it was warm in these four walls.

Still, keeping up with their escapees was of the utmost importance. So, once they'd given Blanca an hour's rest, they started gathering their things again, Axel dousing the fire, Selena putting Blanca's supplies back in her pack.

She adjusted her hood on her head, and Axel placed the silly headlamp over his stocking cap. Why didn't it look silly on him? Something about the square jaw or sharp nose. *Or just the fact he's a hot guy.*

"How long do you think they can last out there without supplies?" Selena asked. Maybe the cold wouldn't be so bad. She wouldn't be tempted to study his face when the wind felt like knives against her exposed skin.

"We don't know what they might have taken from that cabin," Axel said, adjusting the pack on his back, then eyeing the shack to make sure they hadn't left anything behind.

"Could something have been *left* at the cabin for them?"

Axel was quiet as he opened the door and they stepped back out into the icy chill of a February night.

"Interesting thought," he said after a while. "I'm hoping the owner of the cabin gives us some clues as to that, but for now..."

"For now, we march."

"You know, some people do this for fun."

"Chase criminals through the arctic tundra?"

Axel chuckled, a low, grumbly sound that had no business making her stomach flutter helplessly. What *was* that? She was a sane woman. A sane woman who'd gone down this particularly stupid road before. She'd learned her lessons, sworn an oath to herself up and down, and she *loved* her job more than anything else.

So, why did it feel like Axel Morrow threatened all that?

"Winter night hikes. Full moon. Starlight. Some people find it exhilarating."

"Some people need their heads examined. It's *freezing.*" She'd thought the cold would be bearable, but her feet felt like ice blocks, and when the wind blew just hard enough, it made her eyes water and her teeth want to chatter.

Pretty? Sure. The stars through the bare tree branches were something else—something she didn't see in town—and the dark of the forest was an eerie kind of moody that she got a kick out of. But she'd much rather be cozied up next to a fire looking at it all through a window with heat blasting over her feet.

Blanca sniffed the ground. It took a few tries for her to pick up the trail they'd left behind. With the snow and the wind and the dark, it was harder to keep track of. But the rest had done the dog some good, and though they had to pause and reset on occasion, they were continuously moving forward. Selena following Blanca, Axel behind her.

They were quiet as they walked, which Selena knew was for the best. They had to listen for potential danger, pay attention to Blanca's cues. But she wished she could talk to him if only to keep her mind off the cold.

It was a trick of the trade when it came to long, monotonous searches, stakeouts and waiting. So much waiting in this job. But she didn't usually have to be quite so cold.

Look it as a challenge, she ordered herself. She liked a challenge. Relished proving to herself she could do more than she thought. She could be silent, frozen and strong.

She listened to the whistle of the wind, Blanca's panting, the crunching sound of their feet on snow. "Do people really find this exhilarating?" she muttered.

Again that dark chuckle. "There's no accounting for what people find exhilarating."

He really had to stop saying that word. It made nerve endings she'd purposefully forgotten about spring to life, all crackling energy. Wanting to be *exhilarated*.

They stepped into a clearing, both slowing their pace and listening and watching with great caution. Clearings could be dangerous. Without discussing it, they each clicked off the lights they were carrying.

Selena heard nothing. Saw nothing as she turned in a slow circle. She was about to suggest they turn their lights back on.

"Wait," Axel said, so authoritatively she stopped moving immediately, and Blanca did too, even though Selena hadn't uttered the command.

"What is it?" Selena moved for her weapon, but Axel's large hand closed over her arm. "The northern lights."

She looked up at the fathomless sky to see the pale greenish sparkle that seemed so otherworldly it took her breath away.

They were silent, still for a few moments.

"Haven't you ever seen them before?" he asked, standing way too close since she could feel his breath on her ear. Yet she couldn't pull her gaze from that rippling, colorful light in the middle of the night sky.

She shook her head. "I don't spend much time out of the city." Why not? Why didn't she get away from the buildings and the crowds every once in a while and just…breathe?

"I can see them from my farm sometimes," Axel said, his voice low and sensual in her ear. She could feel warmth emanating from him, which she knew meant he was too close, but she didn't move. She didn't say anything.

"Getting out of the city would do you some good, Lopez," he continued. "And *that* feeling you've got going on—the awe, the peace, the idea that the world is bigger and more amazing than you'd ever imagined—*that's* why people take a night hike through the frozen tundra or whatever you called it."

She didn't fully absorb his words—she was too busy looking at the sky and absorbing the feel of standing here watching this. With him.

"Is it like this all the time?" she wondered aloud before she could think to censor herself. "You just live out in the middle of nowhere and feel this awe?"

"A lot of the time. Other times it's just…quiet. There was a time in my life I didn't want the quiet. The noise, the push, it was better. But you get old enough…"

She scoffed, turning to look at him though he was only a shadow above her shoulder. "You're hardly ancient."

"I've lived a lot of years in thirty-four."

"Mmm." She knew he meant what he'd been through as a child, and she had to admit sometimes he *felt* more than three years older than her. It was the way he held himself. That supervisory part of his job. He was a man who'd either been born older or had come to it honestly after losing his family in such tragic circumstances.

The thought of a boy who'd had his family murdered around him, who'd somehow survived, living alone as a man out in the middle of nowhere on some nonfunctioning farm felt…wrong all of a sudden.

"You need a dog, Morrow. You make that quiet sound far too lonely."

Though she couldn't make out his face, she could sense he stared down at her. She could sense them measuring each other up, even in only shadow.

Maybe that was why she didn't move away. It was dark. She could pretend that this spiraling, *exhilarating* feeling inside her chest wasn't about him—a man she worked with. But instead just a shadow. Someone removed from TCD and the FBI.

"Maybe I need more than a dog," he murmured.

Her breath caught, and it felt like her heart mirrored the movement. A sharp beat followed by a holding moment where she thought about all the implications of what that might mean.

But she'd been here before. All those what-ifs used like promises. She couldn't believe them, no matter how different Axel felt. Older, wiser—she didn't make the same mistakes twice.

She just wished he'd *feel* like a mistake, instead of something she wanted.

"Selena."

His voice was a velvety promise, the northern lights all around them, Blanca waiting patiently in the dark. Their work was hardly done, but it would hardly be ruined by one…

The vibrating buzz of a phone interrupted the quiet, and thank *God* it interrupted her break with sanity. Again.

"Saved by the bell. Twice," she muttered. Because

both times his phone had gone off, interrupting these *moments*, she knew she'd been far too close to giving in. When she'd promised herself never to give in again.

"Morrow," Axel answered his phone, sounding terse and gritty.

It soothed her a *little* that he didn't sound his cool, collected self.

"Well, we've got our lead," Axel said after talking in low tones on the phone. "The cabin belonged to a shell company, but Opaline did some digging and found a connection to Bernard McNally."

"The guy Leonard was arrested with way back when?"

"One and the same. Now to figure out who and where Bernard is."

AXEL COULDN'T SAY what the hell was wrong with him. Working with Selena for four years had been a challenge at times, but it had never truly tested him. Granted, they'd never been quite so alone, so isolated.

He knew all sorts of things about her, but there was something intimate about watching a person see the northern lights for the first time.

Maybe he was delirious from smoke inhalation or some sort of brain hypothermia.

"Friend or enemy?" Selena said into the quiet.

They'd resumed their walking, following Blanca in a line through the clearing and toward another thicket of trees. Axel had to remind himself they were in the middle of an assignment and bring his mind back to what they'd been discussing.

Instead of how easy it was to forget what he was doing the more time he spent around her.

You make that quiet sound far too lonely. The soft, gentle way she'd said that seemed to infect him. He couldn't help but picture her…at his farm. Watching the stars come out on a pretty spring night.

Yeah, right.

"Axel?"

Get it together, man. "Yeah. No. I don't know. Foe seems more likely if they burned the guy's cabin to the ground."

"Why take the time? That's what I can't get over. We'll catch up by morning even with our break. They took time to burn that place down."

"Must have been important."

"To Leonard."

"Seems that way."

They fell into an easy silence, following Blanca through the woods. She seemed to have a good trail now, and he knew that Selena was listening to the world around them just as he was. How far back were they? How much longer would they chase, just out of reach, before they acted?

He checked his phone and the map. Both teams of TCD agents were still a good fifty miles away. The trio couldn't have made it that far yet. As long as they kept it up like this, they'd be able to surround, outnumber and take down the trio without anyone getting hurt.

He hoped for that outcome, even with all the questions about the case still bothering him. He could hope for easy.

Slowly, after hours of walking, a faint hint of light creeped into the woods around them. Selena had turned off her flashlight, and he'd taken off the headlamp and thrown it in his pack. It was still early, dawn just a pearly promise, but it gave them enough sight to walk.

This time it was Selena's phone that buzzed.

"Yeah?" There was a pause. "Opaline, calm down." The words were spoken with some impatience, but also a certain authority that was interesting to note. She was the younger sister, but she was the one more…in control of the situation.

He thought about what she'd said about everyone in her family wanting her to take responsibility for Peter. She was the rock there, and she didn't want to be. Still, when push came to shove, they all turned to her. No matter the bad blood, or the tension, Opaline was calling her with a problem.

Family. A bond even bad feelings couldn't erase. Did Peter have that? Axel knew he himself didn't. He'd watched people have that, wondered how his life might be different if he'd had a family. If he'd had that connection no matter what happened.

But Peter's family connections weren't simply lost by losing his mother. He still had family, but it had been fractured by his father's actions with another family. Gangs were notorious for attracting people who wanted a sense of family, community, purpose.

Had Peter simply fallen into this trio to belong? To feel a part of something? And if that was true, could he be convinced to do worse things than he'd done before? Or was there some breaking point for him?

"They don't know who?" Selena asked carefully, something a little bleak in her eyes, and if the light wasn't playing tricks on him, she'd paled. Quietly he commanded Blanca to stop so they could stop walking for a minute while Selena finished up the phone call.

She stood there, still as a statue, blinking at the ground. When she spoke, she had to clear her throat first. "They found a body in the fire."

Axel's mind flipped through a hundred different scenarios, but he kept his expression neutral. "And there's no ID?"

"Not yet."

She was trying to be strong, but they both knew the body could be Peter's. Unfortunately, the profile he had of Peter Lopez only supported the possibility. A man desperate for family, but not desperate enough to get violent. With two violent men, who'd likely leave him behind in a heartbeat if he didn't fall into line.

"It'll take some time to get the ID. We should keep walking," Selena said. She ordered Blanca to search and started following the dog without waiting for his response. Still, he followed, but he wasn't totally ready to let it drop.

She, on the other hand, was good at letting things drop, burying them under layers of professionalism and cynicism. But he'd seen underneath all that these past few hours more than he ever had.

"Was Opaline upset?" he asked, keeping the query casual.

"In Opaline's world everything is worth getting upset over. Every bad possibility is one to indulge. Instead of just waiting and seeing and dealing with the reality, she has to drama her way through it."

There was a simmering anger there, but Axel could see it was covering up Selena's own fear. A grief she didn't even know for sure she had to feel yet. So, he decided to help her. To focus on the things that made her angry. If Opaline was one of them, so be it.

"Four years you guys have worked together. And unless I'm mistaken, it was your choice to make the move."

"You *are* mistaken, hotshot."

"What? She forced you to take the job?"

"No, of course not. It's nothing to do with her or here. The last department I worked for…" She shrugged, her shoulders jerking restlessly. "Things were messy. Someone was making it messier. I had a choice, I guess. Take Alana's offer and work with my sister, or keep fighting a losing battle. Opaline won out."

"Messy how?"

Selena shrugged again.

"Romantic messy?"

She laughed, but it had a sharp edge of bitterness to it. "There was nothing romantic about it."

"What exactly does that mean?"

"It means I made a stupid mistake, slept with the wrong guy who then used that against me."

The thought of someone using something personal against her, in a professional situation, had his fingers curling into fists. Maybe when they got back after this assignment he'd do some digging into whatever waste of space thought messing with Selena was a good idea.

But for now, he had to focus on the task at hand. Keep Selena's mind off the body until they knew for sure whose it was. "Sounds romantic to me."

"Maybe it was all mean-spirited lust."

"Not for you, it wasn't."

She stopped following Blanca and whirled on him. "How do you know?"

"Because I've got a pretty good handle on you."

"Oh, have you made a little profile about me, Morrow?" she demanded, angling her chin and putting her hands on her hips. All the fear was gone. She was nothing but anger and irritation now.

He probably shouldn't find that attractive. "What's more," he said, ignoring her irritation and demand, "it wouldn't still bother you if there hadn't been feelings attached."

"It doesn't still bother me."

"Then you wouldn't be afraid to kiss me."

The noise she made was neither a laugh nor a shriek nor a grunt. It was some mixture of all three. "Afraid? To *kiss* you? You're accusing me of being afraid to kiss you while we're tracking three escaped criminals, one of whom happens to be my brother?"

He flashed a grin he knew would piss her off—and that would result in one of three things, she'd haul off and hit him. A potential he could live with, though he no doubt she packed a punch. Two, she might kiss him out of spite. He wouldn't complain. Three, she'd march off and they'd keep following Blanca. Not his favorite option, but he'd deal.

"If the shoe fits," he offered, and he decided to add insult to injury and follow Blanca himself, leaving Selena gaping behind him.

Chapter Nine

Selena wanted to strangle him with her bare hands. Or she wanted to kiss the living daylights out of him and saunter away completely and utterly unbothered.

She knew *that* wouldn't happen. No matter how much she prized her control, kissing Axel would be... Well, she'd prefer to consider her other options rather than risk losing herself to *that.*

She considered trying to murder him. Satisfying, but it would take too much time when they had an assignment in front of them.

So her only option and recourse was to find a way to be calm.

Which was part and parcel with her job that she loved. Remaining calm in high-pressure situations. His ridiculous statement was hardly high pressure, but everything surrounding them was.

Too bad it was a lot easier to ignore the barbs of a perp over a man who seemed to have been created *specifically* to torture her in any number of ways.

Because he wasn't like Tom. If she gave in to the

buzz of electricity between them, no matter what happened, she *knew* he wouldn't use it against her like Tom had done. It wasn't who Axel was. Even when she tried to convince herself she'd ruin her career by letting any of the feelings she had for Axel come to the surface, she just…couldn't.

He wouldn't do that to her.

But that didn't make giving in to those feelings safe or right by any means. She didn't want to analyze too deeply all the ways she thought it would be far more dangerous than the disaster with Tom at her last department.

Maybe because your heart would be more involved than your pride this time?

Yeah, she was definitely not thinking about this right now.

So, she walked. She allowed herself some inward fuming, just as she allowed Axel to be the one to follow the closest behind Blanca. Focusing on anger had gotten her through a lot of tough situations. Anger could be controlled. Sadness, grief, worry…those things spiraled out of control.

With anger there was a clear line. She might say the wrong thing, even do the wrong thing, but as long as she wasn't using her fists on someone, she knew she hadn't gone too far. Anger was a safe box within which to act, up to a certain point.

You never knew when you'd gone too far with hurt. With hope. With loss. Life just came and shoved them in your face regardless. You couldn't predict it, fight it, control the tide of it. Which was why she did everything in her power to channel all of those things into *anger*.

She looked at the man hiking in front of her. His broad shoulders, strong back, the easy strides through the snow. He had his hat pulled low against the wind, and still he walked with a strength of purpose as if it wasn't freezing and miserable.

Kiss him? That was hardly all she wanted to do with the man. Which was why she held herself back. Under all that made him nice to look at, and the easy way he had with people wasn't the Napoleon complex, weak-willed, nasty streak that Tom had wallowed in once she'd broken things off.

She was terrified there'd be no breaking *anything* off when it came to Axel. Like loss and grief and hope, wanting someone completely was out of her control.

She wanted no part of it. Even while her body told her all the things she *did* want part of when it came to Axel Morrow.

So, no. No kissing. No more bringing up her past—Peter, Tom, who and whatever. No more looking at the northern lights and hearing that thread of loneliness in his voice and wanting to do something about it.

No. More.

His pace slowed, and Blanca stopped abruptly, a low growl emanating from within her. Selena came to stand next to Axel, ready to think about the real problem, not the stupid ones in her brain.

He pointed at the ground. "Tracks," he murmured.

Selena looked down at them. They weren't just following the scent anymore—they were close enough to see tracks not altered by the wind. It *wasn't* as windy today as it had been yesterday, but the clear indentations spoke to being right on the escapee's heels.

Selena crouched down. She studied the footprints, forced herself to think dispassionately about what she thought she saw. She got down, measured the different marks with her hands, squinted around to determine the wind's effects. She knew how to track people like this—Blanca made it easier, but Selena knew what she was doing even without her dog.

She looked up at Axel, doing everything in her power to mask the relief and hope she felt swelling in her chest. "This is three different sets of footprints."

His eyebrows raised, but that was the only reaction. There was no doubt there, but she felt the need to prove to him she wasn't reaching anyway. Wasn't trying to prove Peter was still alive when that's what she desperately wanted to do.

"Look," she said, pointing out the three different sizes and treads. "One. Two. Three."

"We have to be close," Axel said, scanning the woods around them.

Selena nodded. "Very close." She wanted to rush forward. She wanted to take them down now. She wanted to find Peter and *demand* to know he didn't have anything to do with the body in the burned cabin.

And she hated herself for that very Opaline response. She wanted to let Peter go. He was an escaped convict. She didn't care about him. For years and years she'd tried to convince herself she'd done her part, he'd rebuffed it and she didn't care. She'd washed her hands of it and moved on.

But there always seemed to be a glimmer of that toddler, quiet and sad, standing between her mother and his, while they screamed at each other.

Because if you never face the things that haunt you, Selena, they eat you alive. She hated that Axel's words would come back to her now. That they'd make something shift inside her, a sad realization she'd been fighting for a long time now. She was too hard on Opaline, always, because she was trying to forget that little boy, and Opaline always wanted to bring him to the forefront. And while they fought those things they never addressed, never dealt with, it continued to haunt them both.

"Selena." Axel's voice was gentle, as was the hand he placed on her shoulder.

"I'm fine," she said, probably too sharply, getting to her feet. "It doesn't mean anything. Not really. He could be the murderer. Hell, it could still be him charred to a crisp and his friends picked someone else up along the way. I know it doesn't mean much. I just…" There was a lump forming in her throat. She'd never give in to tears, but she couldn't stop that lump from lodging there.

"It's okay," he said, his hand still on her shoulder, giving it a squeeze that infused her with a warmth she couldn't afford. Not here. Not now. Not with a damn lump in her throat.

She shrugged his hand off. "I don't want you to understand or absolve me," she said, because that was exactly what she wanted. Too much. For *someone* to understand, to tell her she wasn't…all the things she was so afraid she was. Cold. Mean. Wrong.

He shrugged, unbothered. "Too bad. I absolutely understand you, and I absolutely think it and you are *okay*." He looked around again. "Let's fall back a little bit and conference call with the team."

She opened her mouth to argue. *This* close to the escapees, to finding out if Peter was still alive, they should act, but his expression was stone. The kind even an FBI agent didn't get to argue with.

"Two people are already dead on this little path of destruction," he said in that cold voice from before, when the poacher had died. "I won't add either of us to the tally. Fall back."

It was an order. A sharp, decisive one. He could say he wasn't her boss all he wanted, but that was Mr. *Supervisor* right there.

She wished it bothered her more.

Blanca started following him back in the direction they'd come without Selena giving her the command. Selena frowned at both retreating figures.

But there was no recourse here. Much as she *wanted* to move forward, Axel was right. They had to employ caution. The men were armed. Dangerous. She and Axel might have vests and their own guns, but the trio—whoever they were—likely had a better vantage point and certainly knew they were being tracked.

They might not know people were waiting to stop them, so to keep following and lead them into that surprise would be best. Safest.

So all she could do was follow Axel.

AXEL BACKTRACKED UNTIL he found a tight grove of pine trees. He contorted his body, ducking his head against the sticky, snowy needles. "This'll work," he said. Inside the thicket there was a small space. It wasn't much protection, but it would keep them out of sight.

He heard Selena murmuring to Blanca before she shoved her way into the space. She wrinkled her nose. "Smells like Christmas," Selena commented. The haunted look she'd been sporting out there had dissipated back to professional stoicism. It was what the moment needed, but unfortunately it didn't eradicate his sympathy, his…very visceral need to make this okay for her.

"Blanca will guard," Selena added, nodding at the trees. "She won't bark if she senses something, she'll either come in here or let out a low growl depending on the level of threat."

"She's some dog."

Selena's mouth curved slightly in pride. "Yeah."

Axel got out his phone and set up the conference call. It took a while to get everyone connected. He'd patched in Opaline and Alana along with Carly and Aria, and Scott and Max.

"We're tight on their heels. Going to keep giving them space until we've made a good circle around them. Selena found something that we'll want to keep in mind."

"There are three separate tracks in the snow." She looked at the screen in Axel's hand, and Axel could tell she was staring at the little box that was Opaline. "Don't know what it means, of course, but there are still three of them. Whether it's our original three or a new one, we'll have to get close enough to find out."

Opaline let out a long breath. Clearly she wanted to believe the third track was Peter, and Axel found himself wanting to believe that too. For both sisters.

"After this call I want you to do just that," Alana said. "Don't act unless you have a surefire way of bringing them down without injury to yourself. Your purpose this morning is to get close enough to see who our new trio is, if it is new. The better idea we have of who we're dealing with, the better choices we'll make."

Axel nodded, though he didn't like the idea at all. Did it matter *who* was out there *now*, when they'd find out when they all met together? But you never knew what kind of advantage knowing who someone was could give you.

Still, he'd rather keep Selena safe and sound right here until they were ready to act. Which wasn't his job. His job was to be Selena's partner. Not her protector.

Why was that getting harder?

"I already marked our location on the map," Axel said. "Carly and Aria, Scott and Max, you'll want to adjust your locations accordingly and make sure there aren't any holes in the direction they're headed toward."

"I think we're good," Aria said, looking down at what he assumed was the map. "If they keep heading in this same direction, we should be able to have a tight circle around them by…tomorrow morning?"

Axel nodded. "They've taken some breaks, but I'm not sure any of them have stopped to rest. They'll have to eventually."

"I imagine they got some kind of foodstuffs and possibly more weapons from the cabin they burned down," Selena said from beside him. "Enough food and water, they might be able to go on without sleep if they have a destination in mind and someone to meet."

"It's possible," Alana said, her voice cool and calm even over the phone. "From what Rihanna has relayed to me from local law enforcement and fire department, the cabin was well stocked. And purposefully burned to the ground."

"We're still looking into Bernard and what his connection might be to Leonard," Opaline said. Axel gave a sideways glance to Selena, since he could tell Opaline was searching the screen for signs of Selena being in distress.

Did Selena notice that? Did Opaline notice the heartbreak in Selena's eyes? It seemed more and more wrong to him that these sisters would be so antagonistic toward each other when the things that had caused their rift were beyond their own control.

"When do you think we'll have an ID on the body?" Selena asked, and Axel knew she was doing everything in her power to sound robotic and unmoved about the potential answer.

"Hopefully soon," Alana said. "Rihanna will send out an alert to all of you the minute she's got the information. She's at the morgue now waiting. We'll want to reconvene and discuss the information, of course, but I'm hopeful the identity gives us a clue as to what we're dealing with." And if Axel knew his director, which he felt like he did, she knew Selena and Opaline needed to know right away without having to wait for a conference call.

"It doesn't make sense they took the time to burn the cabin," Selena said. "There has to be something more to it."

"I agree," Carly chimed in. "I've read the arson investigator's initial notes—not a formal report yet—but the time it would have taken them to burn that cabin in the way that they did, it's considerable. And seemingly pointless."

"So, there's a point," Max said. "What's the usual reason for arson?"

"Insurance money," Aria offered.

"Kill someone," Selena pointed out.

"Or," Max returned, "destroying something. Sometimes even evidence. Could be there was something there our escapees didn't want anyone to find."

The call went quiet for a few seconds. "Definite possibilities," Alana agreed. "We'll work on that on our end. Those of you in the field, let's concentrate on getting these three men without any injury to us. Axel,

Selena, find out who we're dealing with, but don't act until you're close enough to the others for all six of you to move."

"Yes, ma'am," Axel and Selena murmured at the same time the others on the call did. They offered brief goodbyes, then the phone went dark. Axel shoved it back in his pocket.

He knew what he had to do. He knew Selena wouldn't like it. So, he had to figure out how to play it.

Ah, screw it. "You'll stay here with Blanca. I'll sneak close enough to see who we've got. Then I'll meet you back here." Then he walked out of the tree enclosure before she could argue.

When Blanca began to trot after him, he turned and held out a hand. "Stay. Guard." He had no idea what the actual commands were, and Selena seemed to act like Blanca would only listen to her, but the dog planted her rear in the snow. Looking just like what he needed her to be. A guard dog.

Now, he had to find out what trio they were dealing with. Weapon drawn, Axel moved for the tracks.

Chapter Ten

Selena could take an order. As a law enforcement agent over the years, she'd had to take her fair share of them. And Axel was her superior, no matter how much he didn't want to label it that way.

Still, his order was tough to swallow. He was doing a simple reconnaissance mission. It made sense only one of them went, and it made sense it was him since she should stay with Blanca.

Selena was frustrated, angry and trying to convince herself those were the only two feelings twisting her stomach in knots. But there was an anxiety over Axel's well-being underneath that. One she couldn't afford.

"What the hell *can* I afford these days?" she muttered to herself. And her own voice broke her out of her trance of worry enough to focus on the moment in front of her.

She was going to stand here and wait for Axel because that was his order, which he had given because Alana had ordered him to find the ID of their third man before they went any farther.

Chain of command. There was no getting around it.

Since she was waiting, Selena needed to use the time wisely—give Blanca a drink, a treat and maybe even a rest. She whistled for Blanca, who pushed through the tree branches. If the dog's expression was anything to go by, she wasn't too thrilled by her current circumstances.

Selena got out the waterproof blanket from her pack, the water, the treats. She set up a nice little rest area for Blanca in the middle of the circle of trees. Blanca circled the blanket, then plopped herself down in the middle.

She looked at Selena with the haughtiness of a queen—at least that was Selena's interpretation. Which gave her a smile and helped her keep her mind off how long Axel had been or would be gone.

Blanca drank, ate the treat, then scooted her body closer to Selena. Selena crouched down and scratched the dog's ears, looking into her dark eyes. "I don't know what I'm doing," she whispered to the dog. "Everything feels all jumbled up, and I don't have time for that. I have to keep it together."

Blanca gently licked Selena's face. Some of the tension inside her chest unwound. There was nothing quite like laying all your problems on a dog. Who couldn't talk back and couldn't hold anything against you either.

"I don't even know what to hope for," she murmured to her dog. At the end of the day, Blanca was her *best* friend. The dog was the only being in her life she was

totally honest with. Even as close as Selena had become
with Carly working together, she still held herself back.

She'd learned a long time ago the only way to survive was doing that—holding parts of yourself back.
Hiding them away.

And what had it gotten her? A job she loved, sure.
But a lonely apartment. Distance from every member
of her family. Surface relationships.

Selena blew out a breath and plopped her butt onto
the blanket next to Blanca. She had to fight the urge
to go after Axel just to avoid all these thoughts and
feelings.

*Because if you never face the things that haunt you,
Selena, they eat you alive.*

She thought she'd been strong. Tough. She'd with-
stood a lot of challenges and setbacks and considered
that enough.

But no matter how strong her outer shell, she had the
sinking realization those things she'd pushed away and
never really dealt with *had* eaten her alive. Everything
in her life outside TCD was a shell.

Blanca whined, not in communication but in com-
miseration as she laid her head on Selena's lap.

Selena felt shaky, but she was on a job. She couldn't
indulge in tears. She didn't have time for personal
epiphanies.

Do you ever?

"I don't want it to be Peter," she found herself saying.
No one was here except her and Blanca. Maybe there
could be something cathartic in laying it all out for her

dog. Who wouldn't judge or ask for more. Who would just sit there and absorb. "I don't want him to be dead in that awful way. I don't want him to be a part of any of these murders. I want to go back in time and *force* him to take my help. But you can't do that. You can't force your help on someone, no matter what Opaline or Dad think."

She blew out a breath. She still had a lot of guilt when it came to Peter. She hadn't always been nice or loving like Opaline had been, but she *had* tried. Selena knew in her heart she'd tried. And Opaline had tried in her way.

So maybe she needed to let it go. Peter. Guilt. Expectation. Hope. Maybe when it came to her arguments with Dad and Opaline about Peter, she needed to accept... She'd done everything she could. It was up to Dad and Opaline to accept it.

It wasn't that easy, of course. She stroked Blanca's ears. She couldn't just *accept* it or she already would have. But there was something about...thinking it over, speaking the words out loud even if Blanca had no response, that made the problems take shape.

And with a shape, there was the need to actually solve them. Not just avoid them.

"I want my sister to stop blaming me for Peter. I want her to...care about me as more than just the guardian of things." She thought of what Opaline had said on the phone. Wondering if she'd ever asked for help.

No, Selena wouldn't. Asking for help was like bar-ing your soul. It was admitting you couldn't do it on your own.

She didn't believe she was the sole cause of this problem, but she shared some responsibility. She'd never told Dad or Opaline how she'd felt. She'd either been too angry, or more likely too upset and wanting to lean into anger, or she hadn't wanted to feel…vulnerable.

She never wanted to feel like she had the afternoon she'd walked into her normal childhood and seen her mother screaming at another woman, a little baby with her father's eyes between them. She'd never wanted all that *emotion* choking the room.

Emotion. Betrayal. Hurt. She'd found it anyway. She'd gotten involved with Tom because he was charming and because, she realized uncomfortably, she'd thought he was the kind of guy who couldn't hurt her.

In some ways, he hadn't hurt her heart. But he had hurt her pride. Which very unfortunately led her brain to think about Axel.

"And Axel." She looked out through the tree branches. "I don't want this feeling, but it's there." She nuzzled her cheek against the top of Blanca's head. "Why couldn't he be an accountant or something? Why couldn't we have met at the gym? At a bar?" Not that she spent much time at either—rarely bars, only the gym at work. Maybe if she did she'd find some other person who'd make her feel…

Right. This feeling had persisted for four years because it was ordinary, forgettable, and someone else could inspire it.

It just wasn't an option. Surely Axel thought so too, considering he'd kept his hands relentlessly to himself. Sure, he'd made that crack about her being afraid to kiss him, but it hadn't been so much a dare as…

As…

He'd been trying to keep her mind off Peter. Off her personal connection.

Her heart fluttered obnoxiously in her chest even as her stomach twisted at the thought he knew her, understood her *that* well. And cared enough to use that knowledge and understanding to help her get through the harder parts of this assignment.

Selena swore into Blanca's fur. "I am so screwed," she muttered.

AXEL HEARD THE raised voices after he'd been walking maybe ten minutes. There was some relief to that, that he wasn't spending hours distanced from Selena. They should stick together, but this was a one-person job.

All he had to do was make the ID. That was it. So he paused and listened to the murmurings. Carefully, he moved toward the sounds. He kept himself calm, present, focusing on getting closer to the voices without being heard himself.

He thought of nothing else. Not what it would mean when he identified the trio, not what he might do if caught. Not even the cold that seemed to seep into his bones. He could only let his brain focus on the mission and completing it.

Eventually he eased close to a line of trees. He thought he saw movement but got the impression the men were carefully dressed in camouflage. He stopped behind a tree thick enough to hide him, then carefully peered around the side.

He could make out three men now. They stood close together, making it harder to distinguish between them. Still, Axel was sure they were the fugitives.

"Would you shut up?" one voice demanded in a censoring command. "We know they can't be far behind. And with that damn dog. I don't want to stand here arguing when that dog is on our heels."

"It's a search dog, not an attack dog," a bored voice said. "Calm down."

There was incoherent grumbling. Axel stayed exactly where he was. It would be imperative to observe them without being detected. All three men were likely armed, and though he could probably pick all three off without a problem, that wasn't his assignment. Nor his duty.

As a law enforcement agent, his job was to *enforce* the law, not take it into his own hands. Or take the easiest way out. Apprehension was the goal here. Using his weapon to cause injury was a last resort.

When dealing with murderers, he sometimes had to take the moment to remind himself of that. He didn't believe in rehabilitation when it came to cold-blooded murder, but his job wasn't about his belief. It was about following the law.

He drew his weapon for his own safety and then crouched low. He moved toward the voices, keeping himself as hidden behind tree trunks as he could. He just needed one good visual, then he could retreat and head back for Selena.

Axel was beginning to make out the shape of them. The exact location. He crept closer still, keeping his breath soft and even. It puffed out in front of him, but he finally found a good vantage point behind another tree. Not as thick as the last, but if Axel kept his body angled, it was still good cover.

They were indeed dressed in camouflage, including stocking caps in the same pattern. These weren't the clothes they'd left the prison in. Which meant somewhere along the way they'd had help. Or they'd found clothes at the cabin they'd burned down? Something to file away to think about later.

"Why not kill them?" one of the men said. "Why bother with this chasing game? It's cold and miserable. Kill them. Bad enough we had to mess around with that fire, now—"

"You can't kill them," another voice interrupted, sounding panicked. When he spoke again, he was calmer. "Right now we're just escapees. You kill federal agents, they won't rest until they hunt you down. We just have to evade. Then we really can just…disappear. That's what we want, yeah?"

"You got that info from your sister yet?" the bored-sounding one asked. But he wasn't bored anymore. He was sharp. A leader demanding info from a subordinate.

Axel sucked in a breath, heart ramming against his chest in surprise. *Sister.*

"She's working on it," the voice said. There was a defensiveness to his tone, but that didn't do anything to put Axel at ease.

"What does that mean? It's been too long. She was supposed to give us the intel so we'd know where to go and more important, not go, after we escaped. You're the one who told me that." The angry one. Could that be Steve Jenson?

"That's the whole reason you're here even though I doubted your…mettle." Bored. Leonard Koch?

"She's just in computers, man. Besides, it's going to take her some time to make sure it doesn't come back on her."

Computers. Sister. Opaline?

"I don't care if it comes back on her."

"You should. I have someone in the FBI in my pocket. You should care she stays there." It had to be Peter Lopez. Who else had FBI connections?

"What about the other one?" This was the voice who'd expressed concern over the dog, and who Axel was moderately sure was Steve.

There was a cold silence. Axel couldn't see their faces, though he could see the three of them standing in a circle.

"What's this?" the leader said, his voice deceptively amused. "Secrets? Shame on you, Peter."

Axel had his confirmation. Peter was one of the men here. Sisters and the name weren't a coincidence. He couldn't make out the faces of the other two, but talking about escape, plus the heights matching the descriptions he'd been given, made it clear that these were the original three. Whoever was dead back in that cabin was someone else entirely.

"Pete's been keeping an ace in the hole," the taller man said. Steve Jenson. "He doesn't just have one sister in the FBI. The other one's an actual agent. She's not as easy a mark as the computer one, but I bet we can make her talk."

"And you both kept this from me because why?" The question was calm, even pleasant, but no one— neither the two men standing there nor Axel himself— seemed fooled by the tone. Yeah, this man was clearly the leader. Which meant he was Leonard Koch.

The man Axel assumed was Peter sputtered and stuttered but didn't actually say anything to defend himself.

"Hey, we all need an ace in the hole," Steve said with a shrug. He had a gun in his hand. Leonard had one in each hand. Both of their fingers were on the trigger.

They didn't trust each other. That was good. A fractured team didn't always make the best decisions. Information Axel could use. Or maybe they'd just kill each other right here and end it.

Guilt swept in. Selena could say Peter didn't mean anything to her, but Axel knew the kid did. If he got killed in all this, she'd blame herself. Maybe her family would even unfairly blame her. Axel couldn't hope for it to end in a hail of bullets. He had to work to make sure cooler heads prevailed.

"I could kill you right here, right now for lying to me," Leonard said. Then he jerked his chin toward Peter. "Keep him alive because he's the one with the connections."

Steven paused, seeming to consider Leonard's threat. "Come on, man. I convinced you to bring the kid, didn't I? Because I knew he'd be of some use. Yeah, I didn't give the whole story, but have you given us the whole story about your brother?"

Brother. Axel frowned. There hadn't been any information about Leonard Koch having a brother.

"So, these sisters." Leonard turned slightly toward Peter. His fingers remained poised on the triggers, even if the guns still pointed at the ground. "One is helping you?"

Axel felt shock, true, utter shock slam through him. *Helping* him? No, Opaline was just talking to Peter. Not *helping* him. Had to be.

"Yeah, yeah. She, uh, she's trying to get their game plan. But she's just like a computer geek, you know? It takes her time to get the information."

"Time's up. Call her. Get the info now. From her. Or the other one. I don't care. I want to know exactly where the feds are—not these morons following us, but the one's they've no doubt got set up at the border. You don't get me that in ten minutes, you're dead."

Axel stayed where he was as Peter fumbled with a phone.

It couldn't be true. Surely Opaline wasn't helping Peter. She'd been with TCD for five years. She was…

Peter's sister.

Axel let out a careful breath. He had to push away any emotions he had about the possibility of Opaline betraying them, about making sure Selena's brother didn't end up dead at Leonard's hands. Bottom line, they didn't know where the FBI agents were, so it was possible Opaline was just pretending she was going to get him the info, setting a trap. Maybe Alana even knew about it.

God, he hoped.

"Well?" Leonard demanded when Peter pulled the phone from his ear.

"She didn't answer," he said, sounding…scared.

Axel refused to feel sympathy for him. Maybe he was young, but a man knew the difference between right and wrong.

And Opaline?

He couldn't think about it.

"Try the other sister."

"I don't know her number. I don't remember it. This isn't my phone, you know." There was a mix of whining and anger in his tone.

Leonard shrugged. "Then I guess you're of no use to me. Steven? Take care of him."

Steven stepped forward, lifting his gun to point at

Peter. Axel lifted his own. He couldn't let this man kill Selena's brother.

So he pulled his own trigger before Steven could.

Chapter Eleven

The gunshot was a clear, decisive sound in the otherwise quiet landscape. Selena jerked, and Blanca jumped to her feet.

Immediately, Selena grabbed her weapon. She left the pack. There was no time. She was out of the tree shelter in seconds flat, but she skidded to a halt as she realized Blanca was at her heels.

Whatever was going on, it was no place for a search dog. Swallowing down the fear and nerves, Selena had to find her authoritative and commanding tone. She crouched down and grasped Blanca's collar with a definitive hold.

"Stay," she said clearly, without any waver or shake. "Stay," she repeated. She would have given the command one more time just to be clear, but she knew her voice wouldn't hold.

Another gunshot rang out, quickly followed by another. Selena's heart lurched and she ran toward the sound.

The cold was like needles against her lungs, but it

helped center her. It helped all that training she'd had kick into gear. This wasn't about Axel. It was about getting to and defusing the situation. It was about doing her job. Which involved helping people. Saving people.

Making sure Axel is okay.

He was wearing his vest. He was an excellent agent. If there'd been shooting, it had been...

He wouldn't have shot first. That wasn't the assignment. An agent like Axel being caught? It seemed impossible.

But things happened. Not just mistakes. Bad timing. Wrong place, wrong time. Not enough information to make the right choice.

And she knew the three trying to reach the Canadian border wouldn't hesitate to kill a man. Not when they'd already killed two. Not when freedom lay on the other side. And a Kevlar vest didn't make someone invincible.

A sob tried to fight its way through her throat, but she refused to let it win. She would get to him. Everything would be okay. She was a damn FBI agent—she would make sure of it.

But only if she thought rationally, calmly. She slowed her pace, though it killed her. But going half-cocked into the situation wouldn't help anyone.

She'd run toward the shots, but she hadn't *thought*. She slowed to a walk, surveying the world around her. Trees and white snow. She could see her tracks behind her. Axel should have left some too. She should have followed them.

She could backtrack, but there wasn't time. She sucked in a slow breath of the icy air. She moved forward, because this was the right direction. She kept her pace at a walk, but quick. She slowed her ragged breathing so she could listen.

But the world had gone quiet again. Three gunshots and now quiet.

Selena squeezed the handle of the gun. No use thinking about all the might-have-happends. She had to take this one step at a time.

She slowed, paused, frowned. Were those…footsteps? She looked in the direction she thought she heard the sound. Crouched, and had her gun ready to aim and fire.

But the figure that materialized was solitary. Dressed in black. Tall. Broad.

Axel.

He was running, but not crazed like she had been. He wasn't exactly moving at a leisurely jog, but hardly a life-or-death run.

When he saw her, he didn't stop until he'd moved next to her, crouched in a similar position that she was in and scanned the world in front of them. "No sign of them?" he asked.

But she could only stare at him. Relief might have swamped her, but there was a streak of blood across his cheek, dripping gruesomely down his jaw. His right hand was in much the same shape. Torn-open skin, dripping blood, and he was holding his gun with his left—not his dominant hand.

"You're bleeding." It was perhaps the stupidest thing she could have said in the moment, but it made her heart twist. He was hurt. Maybe not dead, but he was still hurt.

"I'm on my own two feet," he said, his voice calm. Reassuring. But blood was dripping *off* him. "I took one of them down, and the other two took off after getting a few shots on me. I could have followed, but they had a better vantage point. Would have been too easy to pick me off."

"The other…" But she couldn't make sense of that when he was crouching next to her, breathing hard and *bleeding*. "Your face. Your hand."

He finally turned to look at her. "I'm alive, Selena. And so is Peter."

She wasn't sure what she felt at that news. Relief wasn't the right word, but disappointment wasn't either. Besides, feelings didn't matter. Not when Axel was bleeding.

She stood to her full height, scanning the woods around them. "Shelter. We need shelter."

"If we follow—"

"No." Her heart hammered in her ribs, her pulse a painful throb in her neck, but the word was authoritative and calm. "We have to assess your injuries before we move forward."

"Selena—"

"It's protocol and you know it," she snapped. Though she managed to keep her voice steady, her hand shook as she pulled the phone out of her pocket. There had to be a cabin around here somewhere.

"Selena, I shot one of them. Took him down. We need to update the team and then get back to the scene." He moved to put his hand on her, she was pretty sure, but he seemed to realize it was torn up and bloody and stopped himself. "You can't tell them about my injuries."

"Axel—"

"They'll pull me. You know they will. All I need is a few bandages and I'll be fine."

"Your shooting hand… Axel, you could have some serious damage."

"Do I sound like I'm in agonizing pain?"

She didn't say anything, because she didn't *want* to admit he *seemed* fine, even when she could see he most assuredly wasn't.

"We'll go back and get the packs and Blanca. You'll call Alana while we do. We'll update them, see if they can get local law enforcement out in case the one I shot needs medical attention. I imagine we'll still get there before they do."

"Axel…" She didn't know what to say. She didn't think he should be hiking around with blood dripping off him, but he was right about acting like it was just… scratches at most.

Still, when Axel started walking back toward the way Selena had come, Selena had to follow.

"Tell me what happened."

There was nothing but silence as they walked, following Selena's hurried footsteps in the snow.

"Axel. Tell me what happened."

"A lot," he muttered. "Call Alana. Don't mention my injuries. Tell her we had a run-in. I shot one of their men—"

"Axel, she's going to want that information from you."

"Then we'll wait until I can slap a bandage on my face," he muttered, still striding purposefully through the snow.

She grabbed his arm, making sure it was his left, and whirled him around to face her. "You need to get bandaged up. You need to tell me what happened."

His expression was… Well, not as in control as she'd thought. Something had rattled him back there, and she didn't think it was shooting one of the men.

He gestured helplessly. *Helplessly.* It made her heart twist and dread sink like a rock in her stomach. "What is it, Axel?"

"Peter's been in contact with Opaline."

Selena blinked at the ragged note in Axel's voice. "In contact… Since…?"

Axel nodded. "At least that's what he made it sound like. They were using him because he had connection to people who worked with the FBI. They expected him to call Opaline and get information on where we were located so they could avoid us."

Selena couldn't wrap her head around the words. "She wouldn't…"

"No, she wouldn't," Axel agreed. But neither of them sounded convinced.

"We need…" She had to push away all the uncertainty, all the fear and worry. The gruesome look of Axel's bloody hand. There was only thing that could matter right now.

The assignment.

THEY WALKED IN silence from then on out. When they reached where Selena had left their packs, Blanca was waiting patiently. After Selena motioned, giving her the permission to move, she bounded toward Axel. She pressed her furry body against his legs and whined.

Axel could only stare down at the dog. Expressing some kind of sympathy or concern…for him.

Selena disappeared into the trees, then returned with both their packs. She was already rummaging around in one, likely for the first aid kit. When she pulled it out, she still didn't look at him.

He tried not to think too deeply at how much his minor injuries seemed to bother her. What that might mean. In the moment, it couldn't mean anything.

"Patch up my face so we can call in," he said gruffly.

She frowned and gestured at his throbbing hand. "Your hand—"

"Patch up my face so we can call in," he repeated. "We'll go from there." The damage was painful, and he'd likely need some professional medical attention eventually, but he could deal for a few days. He had to.

"I want you to walk me through it. Step by step," she

said, opening the kit and getting out what she would need. When she had everything, she stepped toward him and then hesitated.

"You're too tall."

His mouth curved. "Not a complaint I usually get."

It got an eye roll out of her, which was nice.

"Get on your knees. Put that hurt hand in the snow. I don't know if that'll help any, but the cold can't hurt."

He did as he was told, kneeling before her and plunging the injured hand into the icy cold of the snow. He sucked in a breath and tried to enjoy the interesting position of kneeling in front of Selena Lopez.

But she touched his face with a disinfectant wipe and the burning pain was the only thing he could pay attention to. Since he didn't want to embarrass himself by cursing up a blue streak or wincing away from what had to be done, he focused on his breathing. On the blue of the sky above them.

He told her what happened in quick, succinct summary.

"This might need stitches," she said, unwrapping a bandage with hands that weren't quite steady. "You were shot in the *face*."

"The bullet *grazed* my face. And, hey, it's not the first time. I'm old hat at this."

She paused, then instead of smoothing the bandage over his wound, gently touched her hand to his good cheek. Her expression went heartbreakingly sad. Not just sympathy or pity—that he could have ignored, shrugged away.

This was care. It tightened his chest, and for a few seconds the radiating pain in his body seemed to dissipate.

"Ax…" She squeezed her eyes shut, pulling her hand away. She swallowed, wiping at the cut again. "Why would you take a risk like that?"

"I don't plan on witnessing any more cold-blooded murders in my life, Selena."

"You didn't have to—"

He reached up and curled his fingers around her wrist, needing her to understand that this didn't lie on her shoulders. Not the way she was thinking. "It would have been wrong to let them kill Peter. No matter the circumstances, it would have been wrong. It's what I had to do."

She let out a shaky breath, then nodded. He released her hand, and she smoothed the bandage over his cheek. It hurt all over again, but he'd survived worse. He'd survived a hell of a lot worse.

"Now—"

But he was silenced by her mouth on his. Her lips were soft, her hands cupping his face softer. This wasn't the sexual attraction that often crackled between them that they were so good at ignoring. The kiss spoke of fear and relief, care and…

He would have said hope, but she ended the kiss abruptly, stepping back and away from him. Her usual wariness was back in her expression, even as his body struggled to catch up.

Selena Lopez had *kissed* him, and not in the sort of

way he'd rarely allowed himself to fantasize about. No explosion. No argument that led to the bedroom. She'd cleaned him up and kissed him like he mattered to her.

Then she shut it all away, assessing him coolly. "Well, your face is bandaged up. I don't know what to do about your hand. We need to call it in and then get you to some shelter."

His heart was beating so loudly in his ears it was a miracle he heard her at all. But since he did, some of that emotion and reaction faded quickly. He got to his feet. "I don't need—"

"We need to get your hand seriously bandaged. I can't do it out here." She handed him some gauze. "Try to hold that to the worst of the bleeding. We need shelter, and you need a meal and some rest. That's final, or when we call in, I tell them to medevac you out."

His eyes narrowed. "You're not in charge."

She cocked her head, fisting her hands on her hips. Her eyes flashed with temper and something else he couldn't pinpoint. "I didn't think you were either."

"Touché."

She shrugged her pack on, then held his out for him. When he tried to take it from her, she shook her head.

"You don't need to help me with my pack."

"Have you seen your mangled hand?"

Muttering irritation to himself, he turned around and let her help slide the pack onto his shoulders without jostling his, yes, big, mangled hand.

He moved to get his phone out of his pocket, but he reached with the right hand and hissed out a breath.

Nothing was going to be easy without his dominant hand.

"I'll call. I'll say Blanca needs a break and we need the closest cabin they can find. Then I'll hand the phone over to you and you can report what happened." She already had the phone out.

He wanted to argue, to put himself back into the lead in this, but he also needed to keep his injuries as much a secret as he could. He wouldn't be pulled off this case. Not now.

Selena marched, following their footprints, back to the scene of the shooting. Blanca stayed close to Axel.

"Alana, hi. A few updates. First, Blanca needs a rest. A couple hours of real rest. Axel overheard them fighting, and we know that they know we're on their tail. Let's give them a chance to make their own mistakes. Can you get Opaline to track our GPS and tell us the closest available shelter?"

Whatever Alana said in response, Axel couldn't hear. Axel didn't bring up they couldn't trust Opaline. He wasn't any more ready to deal with it than Selena. But, he'd discuss it with Alana once it was his turn to talk.

"I'll hand it over to him to give you a heads-up on what he found." She handed the phone back to him without looking at him. Her jaw was set, her expression fierce.

She was going to march him to a cabin if she had to force one to materialize out of her own sheer will.

"Alana," Axel greeted. He launched into an explanation of what he'd seen, heard and done, leaving out only the fact he'd been shot and the conversation about Opaline. He made sure to emphasize there was dissent among the ranks. No one was following Leonard blindly, and there was a lot of mistrust among the three. They could use that in their favor.

"You're hurt," Alana said flatly.

Axel was taken aback that she had somehow ascertained that. But he couldn't let his surprise show or she might figure out just how much. "It's just a scratch. And it's worth it for the information I got. Alana, I'd like to speak with just you on the line. Just you."

There was a pause. "All right. Hold on." The line went dead for a few minutes, and Axel continued to tromp after Selena.

"All right. I'm in my office. No one else is on the line. What's so important and private you can't tell the team?"

Axel explained everything he'd heard about Peter and Opaline's potential involvement. It was hard to get the words out. Hard to fight for objectivity.

"It's possible Peter was lying," Alana said. She masked her reaction quite well, but there was something about the careful way she spoke Axel knew was a reaction in and of itself. And she certainly wasn't aware Opaline had been in contact with Peter. "To seem useful or valuable to the other two?"

"It's possible," Axel agreed.

Alana sighed. "But less probable."

"They didn't seem to know where we were. Peter

acted like Opaline was low on the totem pole and didn't know anything, when we know that isn't true. It's possible Opaline has talked to him but downplayed what she knew."

"It's possible. But she didn't inform me."

Axel slid a look at Selena. Her gaze was on the terrain in front of them. He knew she was bothered, concerned, hurt and a whole slew of other things, but her expression was mostly stoic.

But that couldn't matter. "There's more. Steve mentioned Leonard had a brother. We don't have any intel on that, do we?"

"No. I'll put Opaline…" Alana trailed off. Though she didn't sigh into the line, there was a pregnant pause. "I'll have Amanda look into it," Alana finally said, speaking of her assistant. "And I'm going to sit down and have a conversation with Opaline, but until the situation with her is satisfactorily handled, no one moves on this group. We keep them in our sights, but absolutely *no one* moves. Got it?"

It was like a series of blows that kept landing. That one of their team might be working against them, and now they had to take precautions for that over finishing the mission. Still, there was no other choice when the safety of the team was at stake. "Yes, ma'am."

"Axel… If Opaline tells you where this cabin is, we don't know for sure you and Selena will be safe there. Nothing is for sure until we get to the bottom of this possibility."

Axel eyed Selena's back, so straight even as she struggled to walk through the deep snow.

"We'll take that chance. Can you get local law enforcement to check out…" Axel trailed off as they came to the clearing where the trio had been. There was a body, seated against a tree. He didn't move, and his open eyes saw nothing.

"You'll want to mark our location and send out a medical examiner," Axel said flatly. "The man I shot is dead."

Chapter Twelve

"You shot him in the head?" Selena said, blinking at the man in the snow. She'd seen her fair share of dead bodies, but she couldn't believe…

"No. I shot him in the leg." Axel pointed at the man's leg, where there was indeed another wound. "Leonard must have executed him."

"But why…" Of course she knew the reasons why. She just couldn't wrap her brain around them in these first moments.

"Couldn't keep up with them with a bullet in his leg," Axel said, his voice devoid of any emotion or inflection. "His use didn't outweigh his holding them back." Axel frowned, turning in a slow circle and scanning the trees around them. "They ran away when I shot. They were shooting at me, sure, but they were retreating. Why come back?"

It was Selena's turn to verbalize the answer they both already knew. "He'd talk. He knew their plans. They had to come back and make sure he couldn't."

Axel nodded grimly.

"It's not your fault."

"No, it isn't," he agreed, but his agreement didn't *feel* like one.

"So why do you look like you're blaming yourself?"

"Have you ever taken a life, Selena?"

She inhaled sharply, the words hitting their intended target. "No. But you didn't either. Leonard or Peter killed him. Not you."

Axel shrugged. "I think it could be argued that I started the chain of events that led to it. Justified or not, it has an effect. It's a part of it."

"A mangled hand also has an effect," she said crisply. She wouldn't let him linger on this. They had to move, or he might as well have been medically re-moved from the assignment. "There's nothing we can do here. Alana will send in the ME. Come on. Amanda sent me coordinates for a nearby cabin. She said half-hour walk, tops." Which Selena knew meant Alana hadn't trusted Opaline enough to handle finding them potential shelter.

Selena looked at Axel's hand. She didn't know what to do about it. He needed…stitches for sure. At the *very* least. There was no way to effectively field dress it to stop the bleeding. "You're losing a lot of blood."

He looked down at the bloody gauze he clutched in his hand. "Some of it's stopped."

She didn't believe him, at all, but they had to get away from the lifeless body of Steve Jenson. So, she looked at her phone and the map Amanda had pro-grammed into the GPS for her. Instead of Opaline.

Opaline. She didn't want to think about her sister. So she focused on each step. She glanced back at Axel. Blanca was walking by his side as if she was protecting him. Some doggie sense that he was hurt.

It was easy not to think about kissing him back there. There were dead men, the possibility her sister was *helping* Peter, and even if she wasn't expressly helping him the very real possibility Opaline would lose her job over whatever she *had* done and kept to herself. Then there was Axel's hand. And the interminable walk to shelter.

So, no, whenever her mind drifted back to that ridiculous, *intimate* touch of lips that she'd initiated in some fit of…softhearted stupidity, it was easily shoved away again.

No matter how much she worried about Axel's hand, she couldn't imagine partnering with anyone else at this point. There was too much… He understood. The shock of Opaline being involved. The thorny connections between her, Opaline *and* Peter. Besides, he'd heard everything the men had said. Infighting and Leonard having a brother. It all added up to someone who was in the thick of things, who'd know how to proceed.

She kept herself from looking back at him. Examining his still-injured hand wouldn't change anything. They had to keep moving forward. It was the only way to end this.

They were silent as they hiked. Selena followed the directions on her phone, Blanca kept close to Axel's side and there were no sounds in the snow-covered forest except the occasional rustle of animal or bird.

It was almost meditative. Like the sun and trees worked together to make her breathe easier. Like the physical exertion outside had some special element she'd never find in the gym. She could breathe…deeper than she had in a long time. Despite the danger, frustration and worry around them, she felt more in control. As though she'd been granted new clarity.

When the cabin on the map came into view, Selena stopped short.

"Whoa," Axel said beside her.

This was no rustic hunting cabin, but a pristine, gleaming two-story *getaway*. The wood was a rich reddish hue against the bright white of the snow around it. The shutters were green, and they matched the door. There was a wraparound porch, liberally covered in snow. So, despite its gorgeousness, it wasn't being used right now.

"I think I'm afraid to go in." But that was silly, of course. They had a job to do, and if it meant commandeering this cabin, so be it. Her phone chimed, and she read the message on her screen aloud.

"Owners notified. Okay to break in. Our office will cover damages and cleanup."

"Know how to jimmy a lock?" Axel asked as they moved up onto the porch.

"I'm not going to waste my time with that," Selena muttered. If TCD was footing the bill, she'd get inside the quickest way possible. She eyed the door, then gave it her best skilled kick. Something splintered, but it took another two kicks to get the door swinging open.

"That was hot."

She snorted out a laugh, which loosened the tightening vise in her chest. Everything was a mess, but at least they could still laugh. "You're twisted, Morrow."

He shrugged, and they entered the cabin. Selena immediately slipped off her pack while Axel moved into the dim interior and turned on a lamp. Blanca padded inside after them.

"First things first. We need to get your hand washed up and sanitized." She looked around. The layout was open, and she immediately found the expansive kitchen and nodded him toward it.

Axel let out a low whistle as they passed a giant stone fireplace and hearth. "This makes my house look like a shack."

"It makes my apartment look like a prison." Selena turned on the tap, flipping it toward hot. She'd half expected the water or electricity or *something* to be shut off, but everything was working. "Must be nice to be loaded, huh?"

Axel didn't respond to that. He was eyeing the water dubiously. "How hot are you going to make that?"

"Hot as it can be. Scared?"

"Survived worse," he muttered, but he clearly wasn't too excited about surviving this.

"Stay put," she ordered, waiting for the water to get a little hotter. She searched the lower level of the cabin, found a nice mudroom off to the side. There was even a dog bed in it. A little small for Blanca, but it would do for now. "Blanca." The dog padded over, and Selena pointed to the bed. "Lie down."

The dog obeyed, and Selena knew she'd take a good doze for as long as Selena let her. When she woke up, or when they needed to leave, Selena would feed and water her again. Ideally the rest would do them *all* some good.

She returned to Axel in the kitchen. "Lose the bandage."

"Sure, Nurse Ratched."

She batted her eyelashes at him. "I'm a lot prettier."

"Yeah, you're all right," he grumbled, unraveling the makeshift dressing. He winced as he pulled it completely off.

Selena ignored the lurching of her stomach at the sight. The bullet had passed through the pad of his palm, ripping the flesh open and leaving a gruesome sight of blood, tissue and perhaps the hint of bone. She didn't look close enough to ascertain for sure.

She lowered the pressure on the water, then gingerly took his wrist and moved it under the slow, gentle stream.

"I'm not even sure how you managed to only get shot on the pad of your hand and a graze on your cheek. That's some luck."

"Yeah, some invisible force field of luck since the day I was born."

Her heart pinched at that. She couldn't possibly begin to imagine what he'd been through, and at such a young age. Still, she knew he wouldn't want her to *express* that. He'd survived close to thirty years since, and she imagined he had a handle on his own ghosts.

But that didn't mean she could just turn off the compassion she felt toward him because of it. Because of who he'd become in spite of it.

She blew out a breath and studied the hand, now that the water had washed away a lot of the dried blood. She held his wrist and forearm gently, trying to work out how to wrap the bandage, and lifted her gaze to his. "You know you need medical attention on this," she said, all joking aside. "Lucky or not, been shot and survived before or not, you need serious medical attention."

He held her gaze, a steely glint of determination in the green depths. "And I'll survive a few more days without it."

She pursed her lips. "Can you shoot with your left?"

"Can. Wouldn't risk a sniper situation or anything, but I do all right. Besides, we keep a tight enough circle, if we need that kind of help, Max is the best shot out of all of us."

His hand now disinfected and dried, Selena began bandaging it from the wrist up. She was as gentle as she could manage. Every time he hissed out a breath, she strove to be even more careful. She wrapped layer after layer, wanting not only to stop the bleeding but to make as much padding as she could so he wasn't constantly making the wound worse.

"I look like a mummy," he complained, the first signs of fatigue and grumpiness edging into his voice.

"You want me to kiss it and make it better?" She grinned up at him, hoping to lighten the mood.

But his gaze was serious. "I wouldn't say no."

Her heart bumped unsteadily against her ribs. Because she wanted to. Just like the moment before when she'd let down her guard because emotion had swamped all rational thought. She'd just wanted that…thing she'd been holding herself back from.

It couldn't be now. Maybe…she could think about it after the assignment was done, but it couldn't be now. She finished with the bandage and gently let his hand go.

"We need to conference call. Then we can grab a meal and some rest." Maybe if she stalled here enough, the other two teams could apprehend Leonard and Peter. She'd never once shirked her duty, or hoped someone else had to do the hard parts, but with Axel hurt…

"Don't get soft on me, Lopez."

Irritated he'd seen right through her, she lifted her chin and glared at him. "I wouldn't dare." She jerked her phone out of her pocket and pulled up the app to videoconference with the two teams to the north.

AXEL ACHED INSIDE and out. Bullet wounds. Heart. Other…places. Everything hurt or throbbed or wanted with something he couldn't have…or at least right now. The mission came first.

Max came on the screen, followed by Carly and

Aria in their little box. Selena held the phone so Axel himself was out of frame. Clearly she knew he had to keep the extent of his injures as much on the down low as possible.

Max let out a low whistle. "Where the heck are you two?"

"Finally lucked out," Selena said, and despite the fact Axel could see her knuckles were white from the tension in them, she spoke lightly and easily. "You all talk to Alana?"

"Yeah. Told us to stay put unless we make a visual, and even then to only approach if necessary. You guys got an idea what the holdup is?"

Axel could only see Selena's profile, but she didn't seem to give anything away. "We found one of the men dead and left behind. I think Alana wants to get the body taken care of and a verified ID before we move forward. This just proves how dangerous they are. Not just to us, or passersby, but to each other."

"Right. But what's all this about filtering all info requests through Amanda instead of Opaline?"

This time Selena betrayed *something*, though Axel wasn't sure anyone would be able to notice the minuscule wince on the tiny conference-call video screens. "Opaline was a little overwrought about Peter's involvement and thinking he might be dead. She just needs a break. Have you guys seen anything?"

"Scott's out patrolling the gap we've got between us. He hasn't seen anything."

"By my calculations, they shouldn't be close to us

until tomorrow," Aria said. "I'm not sure I understand why you guys don't just take them down now. Down a man. Surely you two could handle it."

"Alana wants to be more safe than sorry," Axel said decisively. "Leonard has already left a trail of bodies."

"Why are you creeping around out of screen, Morrow?" Carly asked with some suspicion.

Selena gave him a questioning look. Axel sighed. He'd keep his hand behind his back, but there'd be no hiding the bandage on his face. It didn't *look* as bad as it probably was, so that was something.

He gave Selena a little nod and scooted closer to her as she angled the phone to get them both in frame.

"What happened to you?" Max demanded of Axel.

"A scratch. Our focus now is on two things. One, tracking down Bernard McNally. And two, figuring out this mysterious brother of Leonard's that I found out about when they were arguing."

"Funny you bring that up," Carly said calmly, and though she studied Axel through the screen, she didn't let Max or Aria butt in with any questions about his injury. "I was doing a little digging on Leonard while Opaline researched Bernard, then Alana mentioned the brother angle. I dug at the potential connection between the two. I'm still working on irrefutable proof, but so far all evidence points to Bernard McNally being Leonard Koch's brother. Not sure if it's a half brother, stepbrother or just foster situation, but they're connected through family. Somehow. Brother would fit."

Selena shared a look with Axel. Even without proof,

it did fit. But even knowing the relationship still didn't help them figure out what Leonard was trying to accomplish.

"And do we have anything on Bernard McNally or the body found in his cabin?"

"No body ID yet, and not a lot on Bernard. We think there are aliases, but tracking them down has been difficult. Opaline's been working on that arm. I suppose Amanda is now."

"Let's all work on it," Axel said. "There's no way they get to the border by nightfall. Even if they hike through the night, it's unlikely. If they go off course, we'll use Blanca in the morning."

"Resting like this seems…" Aria trailed off.

"Necessary. Smart. For the good and safety for all of us," Axel said, bringing out his rarely used authoritative, brook-no-questioning voice.

Aria looked a bit chagrined, but Max didn't appear convinced. "Something is pretty off here," he said.

Axel didn't want to lie to his friend, wouldn't lie to his colleagues, so he could only give them reassurance, not fact. "Everything is as it needs to be. We'll plan to sit tight tonight unless Alana directs otherwise. Agreed?"

"Agreed," Carly said quickly. Max and Aria were a little more hesitant but eventually concurred.

At some point they might need to know about Opaline, but Alana would want to handle that herself. So, Axel would let her.

If that helped Selena out, so be it.

"Bernard McNally is our primary focus right now. I want to know all aliases, who he is, who he pretends to be. I want us completely armed with everything we can by morning. The more we know, the better chance we have of stopping this before Leonard kills anyone else."

He didn't usually bark out orders like this, but he supposed there wasn't anything *usual* going on right now. "Understood?"

Everyone agreed, and then gave half-hearted good-byes as they cut off the call. Selena shoved the phone in her pocket. Her brows were furrowed, and she seemed to be deep in thought.

"Penny for your thoughts," he offered.

She lifted her gaze to his. Sad and serious. "I want to approach Peter. Alone. Just me and him."

Chapter Thirteen

He didn't laugh. She half expected him to. It was not the smartest plan she'd ever concocted.

But it was *something*.

Axel held her gaze, but he didn't say anything, and it felt like he could see right through her. Like he *knew* this didn't have anything to do with the mission and everything to do with the fact Peter was her brother and she wanted to save him.

Even now.

Are you any better than Opaline?

She couldn't hold his gaze after that popped into her head. She turned to the mess they'd left in bandaging him up. She threw away trash, found a dish towel to wipe the wet counters and desperately tried to find some way to get her professional shell back.

But he'd dissolved it, back there, when he'd let her kiss him as if they hadn't been avoiding it for *years*.

"How do you propose we go about letting that happen?" Axel asked.

She wasn't fooled by his even tone. His eyes said everything his voice didn't. *No way in hell.*

"You have good reason to rest. And do all those things you were talking about with the team. I'll take Blanca and—"

He held up his bandaged hand. "This is what happened the last time we split up."

She wanted to say it wasn't the same, but of course it was the same. Splitting up left them far more vulnerable, especially when her plan was just…personal. She could pretend it was about the assignment—that somehow getting a message to Peter would allow him to escape Leonard's clutches, or bring Leonard down and somehow redeem himself—but deep down she knew she was just grasping at the same old straws. Drowning under the weight of other people's expectations.

"You said they were all fighting. That they didn't trust each other. If we can use that—"

"I get what you're saying, but why not just keep closing in the circle until the six of us can apprehend them without anyone getting hurt?"

Anyone else, she wanted to say, looking at the bandages on his hand and face.

"We might get more information about this Bernard McNally and what he has planned. I've been saying from the beginning, escaping prison in February when you're in northern Michigan just doesn't make sense."

"And you don't think we'll get that information if we apprehend them?"

Selena wanted to present a calm, decisive front. The

stoic agent who didn't care—that woman she'd been back at the offices. But Opaline being involved, Axel getting shot…it was poking holes in all her defenses. In all the ways she usually kept her feelings buried and to herself.

"You said Leonard was going to kill Peter. Because he didn't have a use," Selena managed to choke out. "If Opaline was his use…"

Axel scrubbed a hand over his face. "Listen. If Leonard was going to kill Peter, he would have done it then and there with Steve. He escaped *with* men, when it likely would have been easier to orchestrate alone, for a reason. Just like they broke out now for a reason. I'm not saying he won't kill Peter if it helps whatever his end goal is, I'm just saying I don't think it fits with Leonard's goal right now."

Selena tried to let that ease her worry. Axel wasn't the type of agent to say something simply to mollify her. It had to be the truth. The problem was the truth wasn't *certainty*.

Axel reached out, his hand touched her face. She didn't spend much time dwelling on how much larger her male coworkers were than her. She focused on herself, on being strong and capable regardless of size. But now… His hand was big, and he was so much taller with those broad shoulders and…

She was a federal agent. Not a woman. Not here. Not now.

But his fingers brushed her cheek with the gentleness of a…a… She was afraid to let her brain finish that sentence. Like thoughts would materialize in the ether and she wouldn't be able to fight for herself anymore.

"If you really feel like you need to do this," he said, his fingers on her cheek, his words low and serious. "If you take some time and really work through how and what you hope to accomplish, I go with you. Non-negotiable."

She blinked. *With her.* That was most definitely not what she expected from him, and she didn't know how to… She didn't know…

"But for the next few hours, we take the time to eat and rest. You come up with a plan and we'll go from there."

She swallowed, but it didn't dissolve the lump in her throat. He sighed, fingers sliding off her cheek and then very carefully reaching around her and pulling her toward him. Carefully, gently.

A genuine, friendly, sympathetic, comforting *hug.*

He was warm, steady and still smelled like the fire they'd had in the shack last night. She couldn't seem to hold herself stiff like she knew she should.

When was the last time she'd let someone just hold her, comfort her with nothing more than the shelter of their arms?

She didn't have a clue, and it brought the sting of tears to her eyes. She wouldn't let them *fall*, but it was impossible to fight them completely off. She left her hands at her sides, afraid of what they might do of their own volition if she brought them up to touch. He had the palm of one big hand on the small of her back. He rested his chin on her head, and that had a breath shuddering out of her, sounding far too loud in the quiet room. But she didn't stiffen or pull away. She felt like the warmth of his body was some kind of drug lulling her into complacency, and in that complacency, she rested her head on his shoulder.

She didn't know how long they stood like that. She was half convinced they both dozed off, there on their feet, for a few minutes anyway. In that hazy place, she'd somehow raised her arms to wrap around him, to hold him tight and close as though she could hide away from all that needed to be done.

"You need to rest," she said, not sure why her voice was so thready, why she felt…shaky.

Oh, you know why.

She lifted her head up and dropped her arms. She tried to step away, but his hand remained on her back, a strong, steady pressure keeping her exactly where she was—leaned against him.

"Then we both need to rest," Axel said, his voice a rusty rumble that had her nerve endings tingling to life.

She looked up at him, convinced she would lecture, not get lost in the green of his eyes and the stubble now dotting his jaw. "I wasn't shot," she said, managing—just barely—not to sound like a breathy fool.

"We haven't slept in a long time."

Why did that sound like some kind of sensual invitation when it wasn't? It *wasn't*.

They needed a meal, sleep, and she needed to figure out a way to get to Peter. To hand him a lifeline. If he didn't take it, well, that was his choice. She just…had to offer it. And if Axel was by her side…

She sucked in a breath. It shouldn't feel good. It shouldn't feel necessary. He was her partner on this assignment. She knew how to work with a partner, but that didn't mean she had to depend on them to make her feel like she had a handle on things.

She'd only ever been able to depend on herself for that. Which felt sad with Axel's big hand on her back, holding her so close to him she wanted to give in and lean against him again.

But if she did, she'd lose. She'd lose everything. If she gave in…

What could you gain?

She couldn't listen to that voice. It was the voice that always got her in trouble. That had her trusting people. That had her offering Peter help against her better judgment. That had her moving to TCD thinking she and Opaline might have some sisterly relationship again.

It was the voice that broke her heart, again and again.

So when Axel touched her face again, she shook it off. She couldn't let it linger like some half-reached promise. "I'm not going to pretend we aren't attracted to each other. We've been dancing around that for years, but—"

"I'm not going to pretend attraction is all it is."

She sucked in a breath, and then another. Panic, she convinced herself, was all that she felt. The warmth around her heart, squeezing her chest painfully and beautifully at the same time, was just *panic*.

Not hope.

Even if he felt what she did, that didn't mean it could…mean anything. Go anywhere. She wasn't suited to any of that. She was bad at communicating. She was hard, mean.

Unlovable.

But this wasn't about love. It couldn't be.

And still she didn't move away from his hand on her back, or the soft look in his eyes, or all that *yearning* welling up inside her.

THEY SHOULDN'T BE doing this here. Now. But he was to blame, and Axel didn't know how to stop it.

They had been ordered to stand down, and yes, his hand and cheek throbbed in a mind-numbing kind of pain that was perhaps exacerbating his lack of control.

So damn be it.

"There's more here between us. You know it. I know it. We've pretended there isn't for a long time, but it doesn't go away." He'd kept thinking it would, so much that it had become a habit. Just keep assuming they'd hit some magical point where it didn't feel like some invisible cord tethered them together. "It doesn't go away, Selena. So maybe we address that in the here and now."

She let out one of those shuddery breaths that seriously tested what little control he had left. She was a strong, poised, controlled woman who had almost never showed any signs of weakness in the four years he'd known her.

To see it now sent a powerful bolt of need through him, to match all the other needs tangled up inside him.

"I don't know what you expect to *address* about it." She even tried to lift her chin, do one of those go-to-hell looks she was so good at unleashing on the world. But it fell flat. The only thing it served to do was crack his leash on control.

"This." He hooked his good hand around her neck and pulled her up to meet his mouth. This kiss wasn't soft as hers had been. It spoke more of frustrated attraction than *care*, and any of the many reasons he'd held himself back for *years* dissolved. Into heat. Into need.

Into the strangest, most disorientating sensation that this was exactly what he'd been waiting for, when he hadn't known he'd been *waiting* for anything. Exactly what he needed when he prided himself on being quite self-sufficient. But they were locks clicking into place. Bodies made to fit together. Her and him. Just them.

She didn't resist. That wall was gone. No doubt she'd fought to keep it erected, but some things were meant to be destroyed, and some people were meant to do the destroying. Which was okay. He'd be careful, he promised himself that. No matter what happened, he wouldn't be what her ex had been. *No matter what.*

Her hands came up to his shoulders, her fingers digging into the tense muscles there, as she lifted to her toes and kissed him back with the same need and frustration he'd initiated the kiss with.

It wasn't possible to think about anything else except the feel of her mouth on his, her body pressed up against his. She was soft and sweet, underneath that outer shell of strength and steel. It was the combination, both twined into one woman, that made it feel like this was…unavoidable.

At *some* point the dam was going to break, no matter what they did. It just so happened, the time was now.

He slid his hand down the sexy curve of her back, urged her closer, as if there was any space left to be closer.

Even if one of their phones rang at this point, he didn't think they'd hear it. He certainly wouldn't care. Not when the taste of her melted through him, rearranged something inside him.

He gentled the kiss, not sure he could have articulated *why*, only that he wanted more than just heat and need. Something softer. More lasting. His hand traveled back up the length of her spine to rest on her neck once more. Light. He kissed her with a gentleness he hadn't known himself capable of, his fingers trailing up and down the side of her neck.

His entire body was heat and tension, twined with a pleasure so big and different, he was almost afraid of what came next. Not afraid enough to stop. No, he wanted to wade into this new *thing* and explore it until it was his whole existence.

But that was clearly a mistake, since she pulled her mouth away from his. He could feel the war inside her, because her fingers still dug into his shoulders. She'd found some semblance of reason, but it was fleeting.

He wanted to eradicate *all* sense of reason. Here. Now.

"This is a mistake," she breathed. She kept her gaze averted, her breath coming in uneven puffs. But she held on, and he held on to that.

He wished he could agree with her, make things easy on either of them, but the word *mistake* landed all wrong. A discordant note in a strange new world that was all harmonies. Her in his arms, kissing him with all she was… He could find no mistake in there. Maybe someday he would, but for now, it was only everything. "Selena." He gave her neck a gentle squeeze, trying to get her to look up at him. But she refused.

He pressed a kiss to her temple. "What part of this feels like a mistake?"

Her gaze whipped up to his, arrested. She opened her mouth as if she had an answer, and he braced himself for it.

But none came.

Chapter Fourteen

Selena searched for an answer. An excuse. Anything she could throw at him, or convince herself to let go of him. Anything to douse the curling need inside her.

She tried to think about their assignment, about Opaline, about Peter, but nothing took hold. There was only this man who'd given her some understanding.

"It isn't a mistake," he said, his voice low and grave, like he was delivering bad news. And it *was* bad news. Terrible news. But he kissed her temple again, then her cheek, and no matter how she tried to hold on to the thought that it was bad, feelings crowded thoughts away.

It felt good. It felt right. He was right. Always had been.

She shook her head, trying to remind herself of all the ways this would end badly for her. "We shouldn't. Not here. Not now."

"Probably not," he agreed equitably, but his mouth touched her neck, trailed down the slope of it, and all those protests and reasons and rational thought slid through her mind like smoke.

Her hands were still on his shoulders, holding tight, as she tilted her head to give his mouth better access to her neck. She'd never felt this… It wasn't just that haze of lust, or the want of companionship, touch. There was something deeper.

It scared the hell out of her, and had for a very long time, but he was carefully kissing his way through all her defenses, all her fears. When his mouth returned to hers, she was shaking. She'd have been embarrassed by that show of weakness if she could think straight. But his kisses were like a drug, his hand traveling her body a spell.

It hit her that this wasn't—couldn't be—Axel's norm. He was an agent who prided himself on control and professionalism, and he was shoving that to the side. For her. Because of her. With her.

In that realization, something cracked for her. And then him. The kiss became frenzied. The soft touches were gone, replaced by desperation. They pulled off each other's vests and tumbled to the floor. She tried to be careful of his injuries, but even with only one good hand, it seemed he touched her everywhere, stoking fires, driving this insanity to a fever pitch.

She managed to get his shirt off, then had to help him get hers off. They kicked off their pants, neither quite caring if they were fully divested as long as skin touched skin, body met body.

When they came together, a tangle of clothes and limbs, they both stilled.

"Finally," he murmured into her ear.

Finally. Finally. It echoed in her brain like a chant while he moved inside her, driving her to a waving crest of pleasure she would have thought impossible. But it pulsed through her like light. Like *right*.

She rolled on top of him, seeking more.

They found that more, that release, together.

Selena tried to roll off him, but he only rolled with her, not letting her go. She didn't know how to fight the need to cuddle into him, to hold on to this. She'd been fighting it for so long. *So* long. It had happened. What was the point of still fighting?

His breathing was heavy and steady, and while his arms were still tight around her, as though he hadn't fully drifted into sleep yet, she knew he was getting close. And if she let him fall asleep, she'd give in to the need to fall asleep. Tempting, but tangled in a mix of their clothes, half-naked on the floor of a stranger's cabin in the middle of an assignment, just wasn't going to work for her.

"Come on. You're dead on your feet. Let's get some rest." She wiggled out of his grasp and he finally let her.

He muttered something she couldn't understand, but she pulled her shirt and pants back on while he did the same. Then, with a hesitation that irritated her because it spoke to making this a bigger deal than it could be, she took his hand and led him to one of the bedrooms.

It was odd, using some other person's cabin as their own, but they both needed some food and some rest, and the strangers would be compensated. So, she had to get over her unease. She pulled the covers on the large bed back and gestured Axel to climb in.

He frowned at the bed, but she gave him a little push and he obeyed. He yawned, fumbling with his phone. "Half hour should be good, yeah?"

"Yeah," she agreed, slightly amused at how he fumbled to set his alarm. She stood there. Her body was still warm and lax and relaxed, but her brain was whirling.

Until he reached out and took her hand. He scooted over in the bed, then pulled her down next to him. "Get some sleep, huh?" he murmured, tucking her firmly against him.

It felt so *nice* and *normal*, she wanted to cry. Instead she blinked back the tears and focused on keeping her breathing even. She thought about it—*in, out, slow, calm*—rather than all of the other emotions tumbling through her head.

Axel was asleep in seconds, each moment the tight hold he had on her loosening until it finally went lax. She slid out of his arms and off the bed, pausing to make sure he didn't stir.

He'd set his alarm for thirty minutes. She shook her head. That was hardly long enough after he'd been shot. She carefully took his phone and turned off the alarm. Then she slid out of the room.

She'd eat something, do a little work, then slide back into bed before Axel woke up. Maybe she'd catch a fifteen-minute nap. Let him think she'd slept longer.

Out in the kitchen, Selena poked through the cabinets. She didn't allow herself to think about what had transpired on the floor. It had been…stress relief. A blip. They'd go back to normal.

Her stomach flipped as she thought of the way he'd tucked her against him in bed. Why couldn't she have that with someone she didn't work with?

Because no one would do a very good job of understanding your job, or your strengths, without doing similar work.

"I really don't need that kind of clarity right now, self," she muttered. She found peanut butter and a frozen loaf of bread. She took a few slices out, used the toaster to thaw them, then went to work making peanut butter sandwiches.

When her phone buzzed, she pulled it out of her pocket and answered without looking at the caller. "Lopez," she said quietly so she didn't wake Axel. She licked peanut butter off her thumb as only silence greeted her.

"Selena," Opaline's voice finally ventured. It sounded scratchy and weak.

Selena blinked. She hadn't expected a call from her sister. She didn't know what to do with it when…

"I asked Alana to let me call you and tell you everything rather than you getting it from her," Opaline continued. Selena wasn't sure she'd ever heard her sister sound so…beaten down.

"All right," Selena managed, feeling as though her heart was in a vise.

"I wasn't helping Peter. I need you to know that up front. He thought I was, but I didn't give him any information. I wasn't going to. I just thought if he trusted me, he might tell me what was going on and I might be able to…make sure he didn't end up dead."

"But you didn't tell anyone."

Opaline let out a noisy breath. "No, I didn't. I didn't… I just thought it would be better if I handled it so…"

"So we didn't get involved and use him to end this?" Selena demanded, though she couldn't find her usual anger with her sister.

"I just wanted him to be safe," Opaline whispered.

Selena swallowed. The usual wave of frustration and anger didn't materialize. Selena wanted the same thing. She tried to pretend she didn't. Tried to be over Peter. Tried to blame Opaline for bringing up those feelings she wanted buried. But no matter how she tried, he was still that little boy to her, and she knew that was true for Opaline.

Opaline had been wrong, but she'd done it out of love and care. Love and care. Selena hadn't put much stock in those things in a very long time. Too often, they burned.

Axel's words had dug their way into her soul, though. *If you never face the things that haunt you, Selena, they eat you alive.* She didn't want to be eaten alive anymore. So it was time to stop burying, fighting, ignoring. Selena sucked in a breath. Being truthful, vulnerable with Opaline felt a bit like asking someone to shoot her in the face.

But maybe it was better to face the pain and the

hurt, rather than to keep running from the things she couldn't outrun. "I don't blame you," Selena managed.

"You…don't?"

"You made a mistake. You shouldn't have done it. But I can't blame you. I know you want to help him and he's… He's our brother."

Opaline was quiet on the other end for a while. She clearly didn't know what to say to Selena's change of heart. "Alana's sending me home. I don't know what's going to happen. She said she has to think about it, but I'm not allowed back until she makes her decision."

Selena shouldn't feel sorry for Opaline. She'd made a very big mistake, but maybe instead of holding everything against her family, she could start…cutting them a break. No, not even that. Stop feeling guilty for *wanting* to cut them a break. Maybe she didn't need to hate herself for never fully being able to harden her heart to Peter and Opaline.

"We'll figure it out. We will." And Selena knew Opaline was their best chance to find something when it came to digging through digital files and information. "But while I'm finishing this, I need you to do me a favor. You can do all that tech stuff you usually do from home, can't you?"

"Not all of it, but some of it."

"Keep researching Bernard McNally. He's the key to all this."

"But what am I supposed to do if I find anything? Alana won't like me…butting my nose in."

"If the ends justify the means, she'll be hard-pressed

to hold it against you. You find anything, you email it to *all* of us. Immediately. Okay?"

"O-okay. I guess. Okay. It'll help?"

"I think so."

"Okay. Yeah, I won't sleep till I find something."

Selena breathed out slowly. "And we'll get through this, Opaline. I promise." Because it was time to stop fighting her demons through her family members, and instead work on fighting them together.

"I am sorry, Selena. Really."

There was more to say, but now wasn't the time to say it. "I'm going to do everything I can, okay?" *For both of you.* She always had, but she'd kept it under wraps. Under a layer of blame and guilt. "And when this is all over, we should talk. Really talk."

"Then I guess you'll have to make sure you don't get yourself killed."

"I'll do my best."

"I know we…don't see eye to eye. I know… I've been blaming you, but we're both to blame."

"We are. I agree."

"I love you anyway," Opaline whispered fiercely.

Selena didn't think she would have been able to accept that even a day ago. But something inside her had changed today. "I love you anyway too. 'Bye, Opaline."

"'Bye."

Selena ended the call and closed her eyes, breathing carefully through all the emotional upheaval. When this was over, she'd give herself leave to cry, but for now, she had to stay in control. She had to get this done.

She forced herself to eat, though she didn't feel hungry. She hunted up a plate and put the other sandwich on it and returned to the bedroom Axel was sleeping in.

She put the plate next to his phone on the nightstand and stared down at him in the inky dark. He looked no less strong or big in sleep. In a stranger's bed. He looked more like a statue, something carved to bring out the best features of the subject.

Except his best feature was that good heart of his, and it was definitely going to get her into trouble.

She shook her head and pulled her phone out of her pocket, setting her own alarm for thirty minutes. It'd give him over an hour and her a quick, refreshing nap. Then it would be back to work.

She stared at the bed. Back to work. Except she'd broken all her personal rules with this man, and the way her heart was still all *fluttery*, it really was *all* her personal rules. But that would have to be dealt with later, on her own time. For now, she slid into a stranger's bed, next to Axel Morrow, and slept.

AXEL WOKE UP disoriented and starving. His hand and face throbbed, but it only took him a second or two for his brain to lurch into gear. to remember where he was. What had occurred.

He was in a stranger's bed and there was a woman beside him. She was curled away from him, her dark ponytail a tangled mess on the pillowcase. Her body rose and fell with the slow, steady rhythm of her breathing.

Axel rubbed a hand over his chest where a tight sensation seemed lodged. He'd crossed a few lines he'd never imagined he'd cross, and he didn't even know how to feel badly about it. It had built up too long.

Timing was a hell of a thing.

But it wasn't simple, that was for sure. He wasn't conceited enough to think she'd wake up ready and willing to just *be together*. No, that wasn't Selena's way. She might have given in for a moment, but she'd build that wall back.

And you'll just have to tear it down again.

There was a part of him that didn't want to. That wanted to let her build her barriers, and step back into his own walls. They were comfortable. He figured he was a little more aware of his than Selena was of hers if only because he'd had to deal with a lot of his stuff head-on and she'd clearly avoided, denied and compartmentalized her stuff. But awareness didn't mean a person didn't *like* the safety of their own walls.

But there was something here, something he didn't fully understand and didn't have the time to parse, that made returning to the way they'd been ignoring each other seem impossible.

She would not agree.

Carefully, he swung out of bed. He frowned at his phone. He'd set the alarm for… He glanced at the woman fast asleep next to him. She'd turned it off. He might have scowled, but he was more interested in the sandwich next to his cell. Peanut butter wouldn't have been his first pick, but it was better than the trail food he had in his pack.

He tucked his phone under his good arm, used his good hand to grab the sandwich and left the plate behind as he quietly moved out of the bedroom. He downed the sandwich, dumped his cell on the couch, then frowned.

She'd turned his alarm off so he could sleep longer. She'd clearly taken the time to make sandwiches, to clean up after herself. He'd bet money on her having done some work too.

"Two can play that game," he muttered. He went back into the room, careful that his footfall was silent and that he moved like a ghost. He picked up her phone from the nightstand on her side of the bed and typed in the department code. He turned off her alarm.

See how she liked it.

He didn't let himself linger. They would, at some point, hash this all out. Linger in some of the feelings they'd indulged, but this assignment needed to be finished first. He'd make sure it was soon.

Back in the living room, he decided to make himself comfortable and then do some of his own digging. They'd gotten some new information on all the players, and if Axel could take some time to really comb through it, he might be able to come up with deeper profiles of the three men who'd escaped. It wouldn't magically explain what the endgame was until they understood more about Bernard, but it would help predict Leonard and Peter's movements.

It wasn't too much later when Selena's alarm was supposed to go off, that he heard a quiet, irritable curse and grinned. He was smart enough to wipe the grin off his face as he heard her shuffling around, then walking out of the room. He looked down at his phone and pretended to be absorbed in the information on his screen.

"You turned off my alarm," she accused.

"You turned off mine first." He slowly looked up, and then wished he hadn't. She was…rumpled. Even on the trail she tried to look if not sleek, put together. Rumpled Selena made something painful in his chest catch.

They stayed there, regarding each other, both clearly grappling with emotions. He didn't think Selena was ready to let hers go, and maybe he wasn't either, because he didn't press the matter.

She swallowed hard. "Before we focus on work, we should clear the air."

"Clear the air?" Axel repeated blandly, though nothing inside him felt particularly *bland* at the way she was obviously trying to handle him. Put him into one of her neat little compartments.

I don't think so.

"You won't tell anyone about this."

He tried very hard not to be offended she was *ordering* him not to tell anyone, like he was some randy teenager who'd spread it across school after prom. Or worse, her ex, who'd used a relationship against her in her job.

"Look, I'm not saying you're going to be like my ex or anything," she said as if reading his mind. She even waved a flippant hand, but there was nothing flippant in her eyes. Anxiety and maybe even a little fear. Because some wounds certainly hadn't healed yet.

"I just don't think guys fully understand what it means for a woman. You tell the boys, and things change for me."

Maybe he should let her have her delusions, but surely she understood… "They're going to know, Selena. They're all going to know." She paled, so he hurried on. "Our *friends* are highly trained observers. They're going to see something between us changed."

"It was just once. There's nothing to—"

He stood then, because if he moved maybe he could control his reaction. "Like hell it was."

Chapter Fifteen

Selena's pulse pounded in her neck. Which was stupid, of course. She'd faced down men with guns and all manner of criminals. She wasn't afraid of Axel, of the feelings twirling inside her.

Of everything, some little voice in the back of her mind whispered.

No. She would not be afraid. "Look—"

"No, before you insult me, I want you to think about what you're saying."

"I have thought about what I'm saying," she snapped as he approached her. How could she think about anything else? When she was *supposed* to be thinking about everything else. And how could he want…

Me.

She swallowed at the lump in her throat. She wanted to tell him the truth. *All* her truths, but she couldn't do that and then turn it off and do her job. So, this just couldn't… It just…

Axel fitted his palm to her cheek, and his eyes were too much. She wasn't a coward, but she couldn't quite meet his gaze and stay…strong. She needed to be strong. She had a *job* to do.

"There's something here," he said quietly. "We could go back to ignoring it, but I don't think we'd last as long as we did the first time around. Not knowing how right it feels."

She felt absolutely lost at sea and hated that feeling, that weakness. His bandaged hand came to her other cheek, and it felt like an anchor. How could she let him be her anchor? Hadn't she learned she didn't get one of those?

"Maybe we both need some time to think about it," he said gently. "What it means. How it looks. What we want."

She nodded, a little too fervently, but God, she wanted time. *Needed* time. Away from him, and she wasn't going to get that any time soon.

His hands fell away from her face, and she didn't know why it made her feel downright bereft.

"I've been thinking about the three of them," Axel said, going back to the couch and his phone and his completely normal way of acting. "How they're connected. Why they'd have left together."

She would have been devastated that he could change channels so quickly, so easily, but he rubbed a hand over his chin, something he only ever did when he was agitated.

Thank God.

She let out a long breath, working to change gears too. Later. They would deal with them later. She didn't look forward to it, but at least it gave her the space to breathe.

"You have Leonard," he said, taking a seat on the couch. "A loner for all intents and purposes. Steve, a serial group criminal. He never did anything alone. Then you have Peter…"

"Who desperately wanted to be part of a group." She stood where she was, across the living room. Physical distance would be best for as long as she could manage it.

Axel nodded. "I think Steven and Peter were the group. Friends. Partners. Whatever. Leonard needs more than one guy—for reasons yet to be determined— so he goes to Steve, and Steve makes a case for Peter to go with them. Leonard needs men, so he says okay."

"Then why would Steve go through with killing Peter?"

"Because Leonard told him to. Leonard's the leader. Steve isn't a leader. He does what he's told. He *likes* doing what he's told. Or should I say, *wasn't* a leader, *liked* doing what he was told."

She heard the guilt in his tone. Even though he hadn't killed Steve, who was nothing but a criminal to Axel, he hadn't worked through the blame he felt. She didn't understand why he'd hold himself responsible. She wouldn't *let* him hold himself responsible. "You shouldn't feel guilty."

"Guilt's a tricky thing. I've learned how to deal with it, but it takes time. Luckily I've got about twenty-five plus years' worth of learning to take that time."

Twenty-five plus… Surely he didn't mean the murder of his family. But more than twenty-five would have put him at a child and… "But you couldn't possibly feel guilty about what happened to your family."

"Of course I did."

"You were seven."

"And I was there. I really have…moved on from that. It took a lot of therapy and maturing and whatnot, but… The thing about guilt is it allows you to think there was some way to make the world make sense, if you'd only moved through the right steps. Things wouldn't be this bad, you wouldn't have to feel this awful, but at some point you have to accept you had no power."

It shouldn't hit close to home. Not when he was talking about his family being murdered around him and she'd just had to survive some family drama and betrayal, but something about his words made things in her chest shift, rearrange. Things that had been heavy and uncomfortable for a very long time.

"Sometimes the world is just…not fair for random reasons you couldn't have predicted or changed or fixed. No matter what you think about that situation, you have to live with the effects. There's no going back." He looked up at her. "I think you might understand the guilt thing a little more than you're willing to acknowledge."

She wanted to be something instead of more wrapped up in him. But he understood. Even though his childhood had been so much more tragic than hers, he didn't act like he won the bad childhood Olympics.

He put them on the same level of understanding and didn't make her feel small.

He made her feel understood. She'd never wanted that. Still didn't. Or so she tried to convince herself.

"There's a lot of guilt involved for kids of broken homes," he said gently.

"Broken homes," she echoed. "It wasn't...broken."

"Your father had an affair that resulted in a child, which, once the news got out, caused your parents to divorce. You had two families, parents who used all three of you as pawns, death, uncertainty and emotional upheaval. No one looked out for you guys."

"We looked out for each other."

"Not good enough. Sorry. Kids aren't emotionally capable of handling all that with aplomb."

"I don't know what this has to do—"

"Peter is a part of that dysfunction. He's searching for the remedy. The thing that fills the holes it created. You went into law enforcement, and so did Opaline, in a way. That didn't fit for him, or he didn't want it to. So, he's looking for the thing that balances the scales."

She didn't like him reading everything so easily. Putting her family into neat little packages. Especially since he was right. "I really don't like when you put on your profiler hat."

He smiled a little. "Noted."

"But if he's...searching," Selena said, thinking of her conversation with Opaline. "He can still be reached. He isn't a lost cause."

"No, I don't think Peter is." Axel tapped his fingers on his leg. "You want to talk to him."

Selena nodded. "A note? A text message? Something. If he knew… If he knew he had some place to belong, even if he had to go to jail for what he'd done…"

"I'd leave the last part out of it and go with the first part."

"So you agree?"

"Sort of," Axel said, pulling a face. "But I think—and you don't know how much I hate myself for thinking this—you need to do it face-to-face."

UNDILUTED SHOCK CROSSED her expression before she blanked it out. "How do we manage that?" she asked, sounding like she'd put her agent hat back on.

"First, we have to catch up to them. Separate them somehow."

"You're really going to…" She didn't finish her sentence, just studied him with her eyebrows drawn so hard together her entire forehead puckered.

"It was your idea," he pointed out.

"Right, but to separate them, *we're* going to have to separate. Which, you know, you got shot up the last time we did that."

He frowned a little. "I'd hardly call it *shot up.*"

"Well, whatever you'd call it, I'm having a hard time wrapping my head around you thinking it's a good idea."

"It's not. It's kind of terrible." He wished he could lie to her, pretend this wasn't *about* her, but there was no point wasting energy to lie. "I agree with you that Peter isn't a lost cause. And there aren't a lot of ways not to shove him into lost cause territory. So, we have to get him away from Leonard and into your orbit. I think we can do that without splitting up. If we come up with a good plan."

Selena seemed to mull that over. She looked around the room, then went over to the kitchen and grabbed something off the counter. She returned with a little pad of paper and a pen.

She drew some circles and some x's. "If we get close enough to everyone," she said, pointing at the circles, "we can use them to create a diversion to Leonard, while I approach Peter and you can be my backup," she said pointing to the x's.

Axel considered it as Blanca padded into the room. She sniffed Selena, then came over to him and rested her head on his leg. "Your dog loves me."

She grunted irritably. "My dog *pities* you and your mangled hand."

It was Axel's turn to grunt irritably. "The plan is solid," he said after working it around in his mind. "But we'll need to get back out there. I imagine they'll stop to rest at night, but we don't know for sure."

Selena nodded, but before they could begin to pack up and move out, both their phones vibrated.

"Alana," they both said together.

Selena blew out a breath and then took a seat next to him. They both held up their phones for the video-conference that was about to happen.

The entire team popped onto their screens. Everyone except Opaline.

"I wanted to give everyone an update," Alana said without preamble. "And get any new information from the team, if there is any."

"I've done a deeper profile of the two remaining men we're dealing with," Axel said to the screen. "I'll be sending it over momentarily. Bottom line, Leonard is the leader of this whole organization, no doubt. Peter Lopez is a pawn at best. I don't think he's dangerous."

Alana's face was expressionless, but Axel felt a bit like an insect being sized up. "You're sure about this?"

And he realized Alana suspected, just a little, that Selena or his feelings for Selena might have impaired his judgment. It would have been insulting if he weren't a little worried about it himself. Still, he was a good profiler. A good agent. He'd connected the dots. "The facts support it, Alana."

When Alana said nothing, Axel continued with his theories. "My primary concern is why Leonard, someone who clearly prefers to work alone, took two men with him to escape prison. Being on his own would have been quicker and been easier to avoid detection. Especially in the wilderness."

"It has to connect to the brother," Selena told the team. "None of their choices make sense unless they're working for someone else, who's working toward a goal we don't understand."

"I agree," Carly said.

"Same," Aria chimed in. "Hiking through this

weather is no joke, and I don't think they're stupid enough to think it would be."

"But we're hitting a brick wall on the brother," Max said, frustration simmering in his tone. "Unless Opaline's found something?"

"Opaline has been taken off the case until further notice," Alana said briskly. "Amanda is doing some digging while also finding someone who can replace Opaline for the time being."

A silence descended. No one asked why, but Axel slid a glance at Selena. She didn't look surprised, only a little sad. As if she'd already been informed that Opaline was off the case.

"Axel and I were discussing the need to move," Selena said, all business. "We've rested. Refueled. Blanca's ready to go. We tighten the circle, all of us. Instead of pushing them toward you guys, we all tighten."

"In the dark?" Carly questioned.

"Yeah, in the dark. We don't know what they're planning, or why they're doing this now. Let's not give them the chance to show us. How long do you think it will take if we all start moving in?"

"A couple hours," Max said.

"So, we move out now. In a couple hours, our circle is tight enough to apprehend both Leonard and Peter, and then one of them will surely be able to turn over on whatever this Bernard McNally is up to."

"They're armed and dangerous," Max pointed out. "We have to acknowledge the fact we may need to use deadly force, *especially* in the dark. In which case we wouldn't get any information."

Axel kept himself from looking for Selena's reaction out of sheer force of will. "Like I said, Leonard's armed and dangerous. Peter isn't. We'll try to split them up as Selena and I come up the rear. We'll want you guys to the north to see if you can get Leonard to follow one path, while we try to get Peter to come back to us."

There was a silence that spoke of dissension, or at least doubt, but no one voiced it. They were trusting Axel to make the call.

Anxiety tightened his chest, but he breathed it away. It *was* the right call. The facts supported the theories, and yeah, feelings were involved, but feelings weren't always the enemy.

"You all have your plan," Alana said, her voice cool and calm and authoritative, but Axel noted a hint of strain in her eyes and figured it had to do with Opaline's choices. "I agree the brother, Bernard, is the missing piece, and we're working on finding it. You'll all be notified immediately of what we find. Make sure you use the walkies once you're in range of each other. Communication is key. It goes without saying we want to avoid loss of life, but if we can't find anything on Bernard McNally on our end, apprehending Leonard Koch and Peter Lopez alive is going to be of the utmost importance to figure this mess out."

Selena let out a slow breath, clearly relieved Alana's orders prioritized keeping everyone alive.

"Let's get this done and get you all home," Alana said firmly.

Everyone agreed and hung up. Axel scratched Blanca's silky ears. "Back out into the cold," he murmured.

Chapter Sixteen

Back out in the cold was right. Night was falling and the temperature was dropping. After their few hours in the nice, heated cabin, in an actual bed, no less, it felt like a cruel slap to be back hiking through the snow.

Still, there was a clear plan now. An end in sight. God, Selena hoped.

They had to hike back to where they'd been when Axel had been shot, then hope Blanca could pick up a scent in the snow. Selena still had the glove from the very first cabin, but it'd be better if Blanca could pick up something new.

"You knew about Opaline," Axel said without preamble as they walked with only the light of his headlamp and her flashlight to guide them.

It didn't *sound* accusing, but she felt accused. Still, she tried to keep her response easy rather than defensive. She didn't have anything to be defensive about. "She called while you were sleeping. With Alana's permission."

"And you didn't think to mention it?"

Selena was glad to be in the dark, because she visibly winced. Maybe she should have told him, but her thoughts had been on ending this. "We were focusing on what was next. It didn't come up. I would have, but Alana mentioned it first."

"But didn't explain. And you'll note, no one asked her to."

"Yeah, because as you pointed out, we're all agents highly trained in observation. I'm guessing they knew it had to do with Peter. They didn't need to ask." And Selena couldn't help but wonder if they found Selena *herself* suspect now too, by association. Maybe the only thing keeping her on the case was being paired with Axel.

Maybe she'd been paired with Axel for *exactly* that reason. She couldn't be trusted with her half brother being one of the escapees no matter what Alana claimed.

"Your brain's working so hard, I can hear it," Axel said, not unkindly. "No one's blaming you, Selena. I doubt anyone's blaming Opaline. The thing about being in law enforcement is it isn't our job to be judge and jury. Your coworkers and friends are going to wait until they have the whole story."

Selena hoped that was true. She wanted to believe it was. She puffed a breath out into the cold. "I don't know what to do with these doubts," she muttered. "I feel like a rookie all over again."

"Dealing with a case that involves your family isn't exactly easy." Before she could be offended or doubt even harder, he continued, "That doesn't mean I think you don't belong here. It just means it's a more complicated situation, and that means it's going to have extra challenges. I happen to have all the faith in the world that you can meet them."

It shouldn't mean so much to her, but it did. His faith. His reassurance. Whether she'd been assigned with him as partner to make sure her association with Peter didn't affect her choices or not, she was glad she'd been partnered with him.

Sex aside, and it had been really good sex.

And it was really not the time to think about it.

"Now, what happened with Opaline?" he asked, gently.

She told him about her phone call with her sister. What Opaline had said. She thought about leaving out the part where she told Opaline to keep investigating Bernard, but then thought better of it. He was her partner out here. She had to trust him and…

She did. He understood her in a way she didn't think anyone in her life did. She cared about him, God help her. And she had to figure out a way to believe he cared about her too. Because Axel Morrow was not a careless man. He didn't do or say things he didn't *mean*.

He wasn't perfect, by any means, but he was a good man.

And once this was all over, maybe she'd figure out what that meant for her, but for right now, she had a job to do.

"Alana didn't fire her right away."

"I'm sure that's a process with a lot of red tape," Selena replied, trying not to let hope choke her.

"Sure, but she would have given Opaline some kind of notice. Just sending her home? I think she's hoping to find a way to just do a suspension or a write-up or something. Which would make sense. This was a specific set of circumstances. Ones that likely won't repeat themselves."

"God, I hope so."

He chuckled at that. They made their way to where he'd last seen the three men. It had been taped off by local authorities and Steve's body had been removed. She could see Axel staring at where Steve's body had been while she worked with Blanca to pick up the scent of their escapees.

She understood Axel too. That was the thing that couldn't be ignored or shoved away no matter how much she tried.

Axel held himself responsible for things. He'd learned how to work through that, but it was a process for him. Of letting that responsibility go. She understood that, because she knew it was something she needed to do when it came to her family.

"He was a man who was going to get himself killed one way or another, Axel," Selena said quietly as she let Blanca sniff around the area, trying to find the right scent. "By his own choices. I know you know that, but I think it helps to hear someone else say it too."

"It does," he said, finally looking away from where Steve's body had been. He didn't look at her, she figured because his headlamp would blind her. But he came to stand next to her. They watched Blanca work, but as they did, his gloved hand slid into hers, their fingers curling together quite naturally.

It felt good and right, and yeah, a little scary, but Selena was used to fear and facing it on the job. Maybe it was time to start applying that to her personal life too.

"One step closer," Axel said quietly as Blanca sniffed a particular spot, and then another, in the way she did when she was getting ready to move. "Eventually, we'll have taken all the steps."

"And then what?" Selena asked.

Axel inhaled. She could tell he wasn't so sure and certain as he liked to pretend. But the pretending gave her some measure of comfort.

"I guess you should come over for dinner."

She wrinkled her nose. "Like…at your farm?"

"Yeah, like at my farm. A dinner, like a date. And maybe some advice on what kind of dog to get. You can bring Blanca and the wine. I'll handle the food."

"Are you seriously…asking me out on a date right here in the middle of the night on assignment?"

"Seems like. So?"

She wanted to laugh, and it felt good to want that. "So, I guess we have to take that one step and then another to get to that bridge."

Axel nodded, and in the faint glow of their lights, she could see his mouth curve. "I guess we should hurry up then."

This time Selena really did laugh. And though her

toes were about frozen through, the rest of her felt warm, and it all centered on where Axel's hand held hers.

After a few more minutes, Blanca gave a short yip. "She's got the scent," Selena announced once Blanca gave the signal.

Axel nodded. "Then, let's move."

He dropped her hand, and that felt like a loss. Especially as they walked and walked and walked in silence, in the dark, and the cold dug deeper and deeper. They listened to the sounds of the night around them and just kept walking no matter how cold or dark it got.

She wasn't sure how many hours they'd walked when Axel held up a hand and pointed to his beam of light in the snow. Footprints. *Clear* footprints.

Selena gave Blanca a touch command to stop, then crouched down to study the footprints with her flashlight. Clear indentations with no sign of the wind softening the edges. The pair couldn't be too far ahead of them. She explained that to Axel, and he nodded.

"I wish we could wait for daylight," Axel muttered. "Too many things can go wrong in the dark."

"Thanks for the pep talk, boss," Selena returned in the same quiet voice.

He gave her a slight grin in the odd light of his headlamp. "Follow?"

She nodded. They couldn't wait for daylight. They simply couldn't wait. This had to end. Because the more it dragged on, the less chance of survival Peter had.

"We stay completely radio silent. I lead, then you

and Blanca follow. If we caught up to them, that means they took a rest. By the way these footprints look, I'd say they're back on the move."

Axel pulled out his phone and typed in a message, likely telling the other agents what they'd found while also pinning it on the map, so they kept their circle around the right area. Once he was done, he nodded at her flashlight. "We stay close. We only need one light. Mine's hands-free."

"Mine's easier to turn off if we need to go dark. Plus, it makes a pretty darn good weapon in a fight. You turn yours off and follow me."

She could tell he didn't like that, but after an internal struggle, he clicked off his lamp. He got behind her. Selena gave Blanca the quiet orders to follow Axel rather than search. The footsteps would be all she needed for right now.

She felt the usual calm wash over her. This was her job. She was good at it. Peter aside, she knew what she was doing with a flashlight in one hand and a gun in the other tracking something. Dark or light, she knew how to come out on the other side of an assignment with all her goals achieved.

The calm led to confidence, and the confidence reminded her that she was a good agent. Maybe she'd been a crappy sister, and maybe she was an uncertain...*whatever* with Axel, but this was something she knew how to do.

She saw bobbing lights ahead and clicked off her flashlight.

"Walkies on," Axel whispered.

They both shrugged off their packs and pulled out the walkies and earpieces. If everyone was in range, they'd be able to move forward. Selena fastened hers to her vest so it was in easy reach. She had to help Axel with his since his right hand was incapacitated and his vest was under his coat.

She didn't let that shake her. He could still shoot with his left, and if everything went the way it should, there would be no shooting needed. Axel with only one good hand was still better than half the agents she knew with both hands in good shape.

They both turned their walkies on and kept their voices low enough not to echo across the quiet forest night.

"Team three in range," Axel said quietly into his comm unit.

"Team two in range," came the first reply.

"Team one in range."

"We want a split," Axel instructed. "Two different diversions. Bigger one from teams one and two. Smaller one from three, so ideally the two escapees split. Team one and two should be designed to attract Koch, and team three set to attract the smaller threat of Lopez."

"We'll turn on all our lights," Aria said. "Between the four of us, it should attract enough attention for them to move closer. Try to determine how many we've got."

"Good, and Selena and I will try to have a conversation that's overheard. We'll take our earpieces out, let the walkie static give us away."

Selena thought about what Axel had told her about Leonard ordering Steve to shoot Peter rather than do it himself. It might have had to do with Steve being the one to convince him to bring Peter, but Selena wondered if it had to do more with power. Or even not wanting to be the person accused of murder. "He'll send Peter toward the voices and tell him to take care of them, yeah?"

Axel nodded. "I think so. He might not come for the lights, but he's not going to come for the voices either. He'll send a subordinate. So, with your lights on, team one and two move in on Koch. We'll stay where we are and try to draw Lopez out."

"Clear," Max's voice said, the other team echoed his clear.

Axel nodded at Selena. They took their earpieces out and adjusted the walkie volume low, so the sound might also draw Peter without being loud enough for someone to make out the words unless they were very close.

"We'll want our conversation to be about Leonard," Axel said. "I think the more we talk about getting him, the more likely he'll be to send Peter to check it out."

"He wouldn't come himself?"

Axel shook his head. "Overhearing the conversation with Leonard, Steve and Peter was more enlightening than any profile could be. I could hear what he said and the way he said it. The way he interacted with the other men. He liked wielding his power. He wants to feel in charge. Like whoever is following him has to jump when he says jump."

Out in the woods, lights began to pop on. Flashlights, clearly carving out swaths of light. It was time to act. Axel started walking toward the center of the circle they'd determined on their maps, motioning Selena to follow. Blanca trotted behind them, still heeding Selena's earlier command to follow.

"I think it's interesting Leonard has clearly taken great pains to distance himself from the brother," Axel said. He didn't shout it, didn't even sound particularly *loud*, but she could tell he was projecting.

"Are we supposed to be scared of this brother of his?" Selena improvised. "Seems like a penny-ante thief if you ask me. What was on his record? Like one arrest?"

Axel grinned at her. "Agree. My expert profiling skills tell me he's just another weak, ineffectual criminal. Not even sure he's worth the jail time or all this effort. But we might as well check it out while we're here."

She pretended to roll her eyes at his boast at expert profiling skills.

"I've got a visual through the night-vision device," Max's voice said from the walkie. "They're arguing. Leonard's pointing in your direction. Keep it up, whatever you're doing. I think he's going to send Peter your way."

THEY CONTINUED TO disparage Bernard, sometimes throwing in a few scathing remarks about Leonard's intelligence. The relationship between Bernard and Leonard beyond brothers of some sort was a mystery, but Axel threw in a few made-up criticisms of Bernard that wouldn't give away how little they knew about the mystery man.

From what Axel understood about Leonard, he wouldn't stand for it. But he'd want someone else to do the work. He wanted to be the head honcho, not the minion.

"Coming your way," Aria said over the walkie. "We're closing in on Leonard."

"Once you're in place, you'll wait for my signal," Axel ordered. They needed to play this carefully. So Peter didn't bolt, so Leonard didn't have a chance to call for reinforcements. But most importantly, so no one got hurt.

Selena made a hand motion that had Blanca sitting on her haunches in the snow. She leaned into him, whispered into his ear. "Listen."

Axel held himself still and did just that. The snap of a twig. A little sigh of breath. So, Peter wasn't carrying a flashlight or anything to help him move through the dark, but he was definitely coming for them.

"You should stay here," Selena said quietly, clearly not trying to be overhead now. "Out of sight with Blanca. So he thinks it's just me."

"He heard both of us."

"I know, but you said yourself I should talk to him alone. I'm not saying you should go away, just stay put. I'll keep my flashlight on, you'll keep us in sight."

"And what do you plan to do?"

"Just try to talk to him. Maybe I can get him to surrender without a fight. I take him, the team of four takes Leonard. Everyone's safe."

Axel hissed out a breath, realizing belatedly he'd curled his injured hand into a fist.

"If he didn't have anything to do with the string of murders…"

Selena trailed off and Axel knew he didn't have to remind her that it was a big *if*.

"Just stay here."

She said it like an order, but there was a question in the way she paused. Axel gave a slight nod. "No more than twenty yards, Lopez. No more."

She began to immediately move. Blanca whined next to Axel, and Axel felt a bit like doing the same. He just wasn't sure this was the right course of action, but he knew Selena needed it. She needed this chance, and she was a good enough agent to know that if it didn't work out, if Peter wasn't persuaded, she'd take him down.

Maybe not with as much force as she would have for a man who wasn't related to her, but she'd still do it. Axel had to believe she would.

Axel kept his eyes on the light, moving carefully in the dark of the woods. She took her time, which gave him some comfort. She wasn't hurrying in, guns blazing, trying to play hero to everyone. She was taking precautions.

His phone buzzed in his pocket, and Axel pulled it out, figuring it would be Alana with an important update on Bernard or even Leonard. He fumbled a bit trying to answer with his bandaged hand, but he wasn't about to put his gun down.

"Morrow."

"Didn't want to put this out over the walkie," Max's voice said, low and determined. "But I can get in place to take Peter out should the need arise. Just as a precaution."

Axel trusted Max's judgment, but it just didn't feel right. He wasn't one hundred percent happy with Selena over there meeting up with Peter, but a sniper in place felt all wrong. "We want them alive."

"We want us alive too."

"Six of us, two of them. We don't need a sniper."

"Selena is awfully close. It wouldn't take much for him to take her hostage, or worse."

"He's not going to hurt her."

"How do you know? I've seen family members do a lot worse than just hurt each other. Haven't you?"

"I've got a gun and I'm closer than you four. If Peter tries something, I can take care of it. That's why I'm here." Of course, he didn't have the night-vision devices the rest of the team had or his best hand available. Still, he trusted Selena to handle this. And if Leonard started toward them, the rest of the team would stop him.

"I'm just saying it wouldn't hurt—"

Axel cut him off. "Sometimes you listen to your gut, Max. A sniper in place is asking for trouble we don't want. Stick with the team and arrest Leonard."

There was a slight pause, as if Max was determining what exactly to say. When he finally spoke, Axel knew it was as a friend, not as a coworker. "*Is* it your gut? Or is it something else?"

It landed like the jab it was, though Axel knew it was concern not accusation. Axel couldn't help but entertain the doubt Max's words brought up. Was he letting something happen because of his feelings for Selena?

But he had to reject that thought. "If this was about that something else, I'd have her locked up in a room while I took care of everything. I'm not going to pretend I didn't have the urge, but we need information, and with Steve Jenson dead, Peter is going to be the best source of that. We can't just think about apprehension—we have to think about handling this in a way that creates an open-and-shut trial."

Max was silent for a few humming seconds again. "All right," he eventually acquiesced.

"Focus on Leonard. We know they were trying to get across the border. They had to be meeting someone there. We have to make sure whoever is waiting for them won't get antsy and come get them. And we have to make sure we can keep Leonard from taking Peter out if he thinks Peter's going to give us information."

"Got it," Max said. "Take care of yourself."

"You too."

Axel was about to shove his phone back in his pocket, but it buzzed again, a text from Opaline that read, URGENT. Axel read the rest of the message, his stomach sinking as though it had turned to lead.

Bernard McNally. Think he's a serial cop killer. Emailing the evidence. BE CAREFUL.

He could see she'd sent the message to everyone. The entire team on the ground, Alana and Amanda, as well.

Axel didn't have time to read the email or the evidence. He looked up at Selena. Her light hadn't moved in a few minutes. He followed where it pointed, and though it didn't illuminate much from this distance, he thought he could make out a pair of shoes in the beam.

She'd found Peter and was talking to him.

"Lopez, we've got a situation," he said into his walkie.

"I thought Opaline was off the case," Carly said, her voice followed by a blast of static. "What's this text and email about? Should we really—"

"Someone tell me what the email says," Axel interrupted, keeping his gaze focused on Selena. Had she turned off her walkie? She certainly wasn't responding as she talked with Peter.

"Opaline tied each of his aliases she found with the murder of a police officer," Aria said, clearly skimming the email and giving the main points. "She says the cases have a pattern. He started with small-town, low-level sheriff's deputies, then moved up to bigger cities, higher ranks." Even over the walkie Axel caught Aria's harsh intake of breath. "The body in Bernard McNally's cabin was an ATF agent."

"No known whereabouts," Carly said. Her voice was

hard, which meant she was rattled. "Which means he could be anywhere. Especially if that cabin was his."

"Clear," Axel muttered. This had just gotten a hell of a lot more complicated. He had to believe Bernard was in Canada, that Leonard and Peter were trying to get there. But the fact the dead body in Bernard's cabin was a government agent…

It spoke of escalation, and it suddenly made Peter—who had two sisters who worked for the FBI—and his involvement with Leonard seem a lot more sinister.

Then, more sinister by far, Selena's light bobbled, jerked and went dark.

Axel stepped forward then forced himself to think before he acted. His light was off, and he'd keep it that way. Without light, he could only make out his team, not Selena or Peter.

Blanca whined from behind him, and Axel crouched next to the dog, focusing on the cool calm of a man on assignment. He couldn't afford to be anything else. "Blanca, I sure hope you're going to listen to orders from me, because you've got to find Selena. Now."

Chapter Seventeen

Selena approached Peter's antsy form. He looked like he was trying to sneak toward her, but he was too… fidgety. Everything a little too jerky to be smooth, undetectable movements.

She turned down the volume on her comm unit. It wasn't exactly standard operating procedure, but she needed to be able to focus on Peter. Besides, Axel would keep her in sight, and if something changed, he or the team would handle it.

She had to handle this. Everything would be fine. It had to be. And she had to give this one shot. If Peter refused, she'd let it go. She'd have to let it go, and the guilt with it. She'd arrest him herself if she had to. That was a promise—to herself, and to her team.

"Peter."

He came up short. She didn't know if he recognized her voice, was surprised to see her here or what. She could just barely make out his face, but surely he knew she'd be one of the people after him. Maybe he just hadn't expected her to catch up.

"Er, where's your dog?"

It wasn't the question she would have expected, and it made her wish she'd brought Blanca with her. She'd feel a bit like a safety net at the moment. Instead of out here in no-man's land alone with her brother, who was acting like they'd just happened to run into each other during a walk in the park.

Peter's gaze dropped to the gun in her hand. She lifted her flashlight so the beam would illuminate him and give her an idea if he was carrying a weapon.

"Did he really send you out here without a light or a gun?" she asked dubiously.

Peter didn't respond. He just looked around, still fidgety and...strange. She wasn't sure how she'd expected him to act, but she didn't understand this.

There was no time to. She moved a little bit closer. He didn't back away, just eyed her warily.

"Peter, I want to help you. I think you know Leonard would throw you under the bus the second he could. *If* you survive. Let me help."

His expression didn't quite curl into its normal sneer, but it was close. "You always say you want to help."

"So, why won't you let me?"

"I don't need your pity help. I'm taking care of things on my own."

She bit back the bitter laugh and tried to keep her tone moderate, without judgment. "Are you?"

He inhaled sharply at that, but he didn't answer or say anything else.

"You're going back to jail. For longer this time. You

had to understand that when you escaped. You might be in there for the rest of your life. But if you come with me, if you give us what you know about Leonard, you've got a chance. A *real* chance to have a life."

"I don't have any chances," Peter said bitterly. But his expression went lax, almost…sad. "Steve was going to…" Peter trailed off, shaking his head. "He would have been fine if not for you guys."

"You mean if not for Leonard Koch. *He's* the one who killed Steve and you know it. Blame Leonard, not us."

Peter didn't shake that away. If anything, his expression kind of crumpled, like a little boy about ready to cry. But he didn't cry, and the sadness was quickly replaced by an edgy anger.

Selena didn't let it fester. She didn't have time to anyway. "Opaline got kicked out of the FBI because of what she did for you," Selena said. It was a slight exaggeration as Opaline hadn't been officially fired, but Selena figured she had reason to exaggerate a little. To try to reach Peter however she could, even through guilt.

Peter's expression shuttered. "She didn't even help me. She just pretended."

"Doesn't matter so much when you keep that pretending a secret from your boss. She's done nothing but try to be there for you. I've tried to help you." But that was anger and guilt talking, and she had to find something else, *hope* something else would get to him.

"We're your family, Peter. We've all made mistakes, but I can help you now. If you let me."

"You don't want to help me."

"I am standing here, my team far away. It's just me and you. If I didn't want to help you, we'd all have surrounded you already and arrested you. We have more men than you. We know where you're headed. It's over for you and Leonard, but if you cooperate, Peter, I *can* help."

"You've got a gun," he said.

She didn't point out that she was a federal agent so of *course* she had a gun. This was dangerous, and God knew even if she let herself trust Peter, she wasn't going to trust Leonard. But this wasn't about her or reasonable action. This was about getting Peter to *listen*.

"You want me to put it down?" She started to crouch to lay the gun down on the ground. Axel and the rest of the team would have her back, and she had to show Peter some evidence of trust. Besides, she could and would fight if she had to.

"No! No, don't do that," he hissed, surprising her so much she paused midcrouch. "You have to get out of here," Peter said. He was scowling, but there was fear under all that bravado. His eyes darted around the woods as if he thought anyone might jump out. Maybe he was afraid of being arrested, but Selena thought maybe…just maybe…he was afraid of Leonard.

"If you surrender yourself, come with me—"

Peter shook his head emphatically. "Too late for that. You have to get out of here. Now. Please."

Her eyebrows drew together as she stared at Peter. She didn't see the little boy she'd known right now. She saw a fidgety, scared guy who'd gotten into something *way* too deep. Who was begging her to get out of here. "Why?" she demanded.

"It's you they want."

He couldn't have said anything that would have confused her more. "Me?"

"Not you specifically, but—"

"That'll be enough, Peter."

Selena whirled at the voice, gun at the ready. But she didn't see anyone. Only darkness.

"D-don't hurt her," Peter said, his voice shaky and pleading. "She's… She won't… There's other ones out there. More important ones. You want an important one. The boss guy. That's who you said you really wanted."

Selena didn't understand what was going on, but she immediately clicked her flashlight off, plunging the entire world around them into darkness. Whoever was out there, Leonard or someone else, was definitely going to kill her if they could. The light gave her away, but not now.

She'd have to disappear into the shadows, find her way back to Axel. *And leave Peter behind?*

And who was the voice? Leonard? But her team was supposed to have their sights on Leonard.

The boss guy. That was Axel. They wanted to kill Axel?

It didn't make sense, so she had to focus on what

did. Getting away from that voice. Getting to Axel and warning him.

With everyone so close, everything so tense, she couldn't risk turning her walkie back up, but she had her earpiece in her pocket. If she could get far enough away that a few rustling noises and clicks wouldn't give away her exact location, she could get that situated.

She tried to give herself a second to orient. Peter had been in front of her, a few yards away. She hadn't been able to tell where the voice had come from. Neither direction nor vicinity to Peter or herself. It felt like it had come out of nowhere.

But thinking like that wasn't going to get her out of this situation. She could see where the rest of the team still had their lights on. Which meant she just had to slowly turn until she saw the slight beam of Axel's light.

If he'd turned it on. If she could get there without making too much noise. If—

Her phone buzzed. She bit back a curse, immediately moving as stealthily as she could in the direction she hoped would lead her to Axel. She pulled the phone out of her pocket, focusing more on those quiet, stealthy steps than the phone at first.

But it buzzed again, the screen brightening up. She fumbled with the switch to completely silence the damn thing, turn it off so it couldn't give off any light, but the message on the screen distracted her for one moment.

URGENT! Bernard McNally. Think he's a serial cop killer. Emailing the evidence. BE CAREFUL.

"You're going to want to heed that warning."

She couldn't bite back the scream that escaped her, or stop herself from fumbling her phone, which then thudded to the ground. She had to run, but the blow came out of nowhere instead and knocked her to the ground.

But she wouldn't go down that easily.

SELENA'S SCREAM MADE Axel's blood run cold.

"Move," Axel yelled into his comm unit. "All bets are off. Just get Selena out of there," he ordered into the walkie. He didn't listen for the answers. He immediately moved in the direction Selena had gone, Blanca at his heels.

Axel kept following Blanca, hoping to God the commands were right or at least enough for Blanca to lead him to Selena.

"Scott has Leonard. We're going dark." It was Aria's voice over the walkie. The lights went out, one by one, until the entire woods were pitched into darkness.

So Axel had to focus on the sounds of the dog moving, focus on following her in the complete and utter black.

Seconds turned into minutes, but Axel only focused on movement. On listening and following. He didn't let his brain go anywhere else. One thing at a time. One step at a time. They'd get to Selena. The dog would get to her owner, and then Axel would get her out of this mess.

He didn't let himself blame himself for allowing her

to get into it in the first place. He'd save that for later, when they were both okay. Each next step would need to be assessed in the moment, so he kept his mind blank of everything except *this* step.

Blanca slowed and gave a slight growl. Axel gripped the gun harder in his left hand. He tried to squint through the dark, but it was no use. He thought of asking for an update from the team, but Blanca had stopped completely.

Surely they were close. To Selena. Or Peter.

Before Axel could decide on the next move, light flooded his surroundings in a blinding flash. Axel instinctually squeezed his eyes shut and flung his arm over his eyes before fighting back the reflex. Where was the light coming from?

Axel blinked through the painful brightness until his eyes adjusted. He frowned at the structure in front of him. Some kind of platform that looked newly constructed. Almost like a stage in the middle of the woods.

He raised his gaze to the figures on the stage, where four poles with bright stadium-esque lights blazed down, illuminating a large man standing at the center, Selena next to him.

"Drop your weapons," the man shouted. He had a gun pressed to Selena's temple. Her expression was furious and defiant, but her arms were behind her back and a trickle of blood dripped from her temple and her mouth.

She'd given him a fight, that was for sure. But her

hands must be bound behind her back. Peter stood a few feet away, fidgeting. Axel couldn't see them, but he knew his team would be approaching, slowly. Tactically.

"You must be Bernard," Axel said, forcing his voice to sound calm. He didn't know this man or how to handle him, and if he got off on killing law enforcement, there'd be no *reasoning* with him. They just had to get Selena out of there, then take him out. Beginning and end of story.

"Axel Morrow, there you are!" he greeted jovially. "I'd drop the gun before I blow her brain matter everywhere."

That wasn't the example he wanted to set for the rest of the team. Still, it would buy him time. Slowly he crouched, making a show out of gently placing his gun on the ground as he spoke into his comm unit. "No matter what he says, at least one person keeps a gun on him. No matter what."

Slowly, Axel stood back up, and looked at Bernard, who was smirking.

"It's your lucky day, Axel Morrow, *supervisory* special agent. Why don't you come join us on the stage?"

"Suicide by cop," Aria said into the walkie. "This is about body count. Not survival *or* his brother. He knows we're out here. He knows even if he kills the both of you, he can't get out of here without going through us."

Axel agreed with the assessment. If he got up on stage, even if he put his weapon down, he'd have a chance to take Bernard down. But surely Bernard wasn't stupid enough to think two FBI agents couldn't stop him if given the chance.

He'd either shoot Axel before he got up on the stage, or there was more here. A bigger, far more danger-ous plan.

Keeping the movement as discreet as possible, and his gaze firmly pinned on Bernard, Axel muttered into his comm unit, "Max, check for explosives." It would be a way to kill them all. If Bernard was already re-solved to his fate, blowing up the whole area would be a way to kill a bunch of agents.

"Got it," Max said. "I'll check under the platform first."

Axel didn't say anything, but he figured Max was right. The platform could be hiding explosives. What other reason was there for it?

"Come on now," Bernard said, the gun still dug hard into Selena's temple. "Don't be shy. Let's get this show on the road. I've been planning for it. Thank you, all, for falling so perfectly into my plan."

Axel kept his expression bland, though fury bubbled under the surface. He wasn't sure how they could have possibly seen this coming, but he couldn't help wish-ing they'd taken some other tactic here.

But there were no do-overs. There was only now, and getting Selena and the rest of his team safe and sound. He couldn't order them to back off, even with the threat of explosives, until they got Selena out of there.

He took a careful step toward the stage, hoping

Blanca would read and obey his "stay" hand command. For the first time, he let his gaze turn fully to Selena. The gun dug into her temple, and the blood was now dripping off her chin.

But when their gazes locked, she winked. *Winked.*

Axel didn't know what on earth to do with that.

Chapter Eighteen

Axel's shock at her winking was visible in his expression for approximately one second before he went back into FBI agent mode.

She couldn't verbalize to him that he was more of a target than she was. She was the bait. But she could give him at least a hint that she wasn't totally out of her element.

Not that Bernard wouldn't kill her. From what she could tell, murder was his only goal. Even if he died in the process. Maybe *especially* if he died in the process. As long as he took out a bunch of agents on his way.

Peter was the outlier. She didn't think he'd hurt her, not when he'd tried to warn her away. But he wasn't helping her either. He was too afraid. Too certain he had no hope.

Or maybe he just didn't care that the big psychopath had beaten up his sister. Maybe he'd even enjoyed it.

Didn't matter.

Selena had kept her head. Bernard had gotten a good few knocks in, but when he'd tied her hands behind her back, she'd managed to keep the bonds looser than they should be. It was taking time to wiggle her hands out because she had to make sure she didn't move any part of her body that he could see.

Once they were free enough, she could kick Bernard's legs out from under him. As long as he didn't catch her wiggling her way out of the bonds.

Right now, Bernard's gaze was firmly on Axel slowly making his way onto the stage. In return, Axel eyed Bernard warily. He moved slowly, and Selena was grateful for it. It gave her more time to work at the bonds on her wrists.

She took a quick look around now that her eyes had adjusted to the light. She could make out Aria and Carly far off in the trees, guns drawn. She didn't see Max or Scott, but they were around somewhere. Probably with Leonard.

"Take all the time you want," Bernard said cheerfully, clearly talking about Axel's interminable approach. "It's not going to change the outcome. Nothing can change the outcome."

Selena fought off the shudder of dread. Her team was out there. They wouldn't shoot Bernard as long as he had a gun to her head. But with two team members missing, it meant they were somewhere out there getting into place. Unless Leonard was posing more of a problem than they'd anticipated.

But Selena wouldn't let herself think like that. Sometimes hope was all a girl had. She'd cling to it.

"Peter?" Bernard yelled, even though Peter was only a few feet away.

Peter shuffled in front of Bernard. He kept his gaze down, patently refusing to look at her. For the first time, Selena felt the true pain of betrayal. He was actually going to let this man kill her if she didn't get out of it herself.

"I tried to help you," she whispered. "You only have yourself to blame for whatever happens."

"Oh, shut up," Bernard muttered. "This boy knows who really cares. Who's really going to help him. Cops and agents and the like just send people to jail. They don't care. They all deserve to die. Peter understands that. Don't you, Peter?"

Peter cleared his throat, still not looking at her. "Yeah, yeah. I do."

Selena couldn't give in to the tears that threatened. Too much was at stake. But it hurt. Even when she should be past it.

"Get the rest of the rope from the bag," Bernard ordered Peter. "Tie Axel Morrow up. You hear that, Axel Morrow? He's going to tie you up. You fight him off, she's dead. Right in front of you. Her blood on your hands, Axel Morrow."

"Why do you keep repeating his name like that?" Selena muttered. "Obsess much?"

Bernard laughed, which made her lungs contract in fear rather than resentment. She didn't think *amusing* him was a good thing in any way, shape or form.

"You and your kind are scum of the earth. This

isn't obsession, it's *justice*. And you led me to it. You and your useless brother have given me exactly what I needed. How does that make you feel?"

Selena hid her revulsion, guilt, fear and every other negative emotion swirling inside her. She kept her expression carefully blank.

"Peter! Stop messing around and get it done!"

Selena winced against the sound of his bellow in her ear. Bernard's hand fisted in her hair roughly, keeping her head still so the gun dug into her temple. "Don't go moving on me. My trigger finger might slip and splatter you all over your friend over there."

His hand tightened, pulling at her hair until she saw stars. Still, she bit back the moan of pain. She'd withstand it. Find a way out of it. Six against one, basically. They had to find a way out of it.

"You know, I might enjoy that," Bernard said, contemplatively. "Watching his expression when it's your brain matter splattering all over him. Yeah, I think—"

"She untied her rope," Peter said, sounding small, but it interrupted Bernard's terrifying string of thoughts. His grip on her hair loosened for a second, but that did nothing to ease the pain.

Peter had just ratted her out. Selena felt the full blast of betrayal. Her one hope and Peter had taken it away from her? She would have glared at him, but she couldn't move her head with Bernard's hand in her hair.

"Untied her… You little…" He didn't let her go, but he didn't pull the trigger either. "No, we'll stick to the plan. Stick to the plan. You'll all die. All of you. Blaze of glory."

Bernard sounded insane, and Selena had to accept there was no reasoning with him. He wanted them dead. Not because of anything they'd done. Simply because of what they were. What they'd dedicated their lives to. Men like him didn't listen to reason.

And it very rarely ended well for the cops at their mercy.

Her only hope of escaping this was taking Bernard down and out. She was going to have to get his hands out of her hair. If she could do that, she had a chance. She could fight him. If he took her out, she could deal with that—if it saved her team.

"Should I tie them back up for you?" Peter asked Bernard, sounding fully subservient. "I think Morrow knows not to move, but she might try to fight you with her hands untied."

"Yes, good job, Peter. Fix her bonds. Then take care of Axel Morrow."

Peter scurried to do just that. He came up beside her, pulled her hands over to him. Which was weird. She didn't know why he wasn't standing directly behind her. This angle wouldn't allow him to tighten them enough.

Then he bent forward, his mouth practically on her ear. She would have headbutted him, but the gun was on the other side of her head and kept her from having any range of motion.

He fiddled with the rope, but he spoke into her ear,

his voice an almost inaudible whisper. "I'm going to push you off."

Push her off? The shock slammed into her like a blow. Push her off the stage? *Save* her?

Hope she shouldn't entertain bubbled up inside her. If he pushed her off, that would be her chance to take Bernard out. If he pushed right, she could be close enough to Axel's gun to grab it and shoot Bernard first.

A risk, but a chance.

It would leave Axel vulnerable in the interim, though. When Peter pushed, who would Bernard target? She needed to communicate with Peter. Tell him which angle to push her out, tell him to give Axel some kind of signal.

Except she couldn't do any of that when Bernard was literally standing right next to them with a gun to her head. If Peter took much longer, Bernard would know Peter was talking to her or he might at least suspect something.

"I've got her," Peter said to Bernard. "Nice and tight now."

"Good," Bernard said. He seemed to pause and consider, then finally let go of her hair. "Good, Peter. You've been an undeniable asset in this. Forget Axel Morrow over there. Bring me the whole bag. It's time to begin."

"Yeah, okay," Peter mumbled, fumbling with Selena's rope as Bernard fully let her go. Though the gun was still pressed to her temple, if Peter gave her a good push, Bernard wouldn't be able to shoot in time. Not at first.

She felt the ropes loosen fully rather than tighten. Peter's mouth was still next to her ear, and he spoke once more.

"He's got a bomb. Run away from here."

A bomb. But she didn't have time to argue, to come up with a better plan that wouldn't get Peter *and* Axel blown up, because Peter gave her a hard shove that had her sailing off the stage and onto the hard, cold, snow-covered ground below.

AXEL WATCHED SELENA tumble off the stage, as if pushed. Pushed. Peter had purposefully pushed her off.

She landed on a tuck and roll, then was quickly up on her feet, holding out her hand. Axel realized she was warning Blanca off running to her.

Peter had pushed her off the stage to *help*. To save her life.

It gave Axel a surge of hope.

But in the next second Bernard's gun whirled on him and before Axel could act, the gun went off. Pain slammed into him and exploded across his chest as he fell backward and crashed onto the stage with enough force he heard some of the wood crack beneath him.

Head pounding, brain rattled, Axel struggled to get a breath in. The pain was excruciating, and he couldn't seem to suck in enough oxygen at first. He gasped and gasped for it before he could remind himself to calm down.

Calm down.

He wasn't dead. Thanks to the vest he wore. Because the bullet had hit him right in the Kevlar vest. He counted off breaths, doing everything to calm himself. He was alive, which meant there was still a chance to get out of this in relatively one piece.

Bernard must not know he was wearing a vest, or maybe was just a bad shot. Either way, it didn't make Axel invincible. He had to get out of here before Bernard shot him in a place that wasn't protected.

He barely heard the voices in his ear. They sounded far away, but his team was yelling words. He tried to make sense of them and move at the same time. Move and breathe. Listen and act.

Focus. Calm. Breathe in, one, two, three. Breathe out, one, two, three.

"No explosives under the stage that I can find." Max's voice.

"There's a bag on the stage," Aria's voice said. "Peter got the rope out of it. But it's big and there's more in there. He's dragging Peter to the bag now. I can't shoot without hitting Peter."

Axel could give no orders, no insight. He could only try to roll off the stage and away from Bernard. He had to get himself out of harm's way and make sure Selena was, as well.

Peter had saved her. Axel hadn't thought it in that moment he'd seen Selena tumbling into the snow, but it had only taken a few seconds—before the bullet had slammed into him—to realize Peter had been getting Selena out of Bernard's grip.

Though Axel was still in excruciating pain, the fog of the wind being knocked out of him started to lift. Someone was yelling. Raving.

Bernard.

"I'll kill them all! I'll kill you all. You'll all die. We'll all die!"

Cop killer. Suicide by cop. There was no getting out of this one without someone getting hurt. Axel would make sure it was Bernard.

"I've got the visual. He's got a bomb in that bag," Aria said. "Take him out. Someone take him out. I can't get an angle."

"Peter's in the way," Max said disgustedly. "From every angle. Bernard knows it, that's why he created that little corner on the stage to hide in. Peter is his body shield."

Axel knew they'd consider going through Peter. Why not? He was part of this after all, but he'd saved Selena. Hard to overlook that.

"I'll get Peter out of the way," Axel managed to rasp into the comm mic. He wouldn't let them consider taking out Peter too. Not when he was right here.

There was arguing, but Axel didn't have time for it. Maybe he wasn't one hundred percent, but he was the closest to Peter. If Max could take out Bernard in seconds, that was all Axel needed. He ripped the earpiece out of his ear and got to his knees.

Bernard was rummaging through the bag, holding Peter in front of him. Max was right. Bernard had built this stage just for this.

It was chilling, how well planned out this all was. How little they'd understood about what Leonard's trio was doing. Not trying to escape. No, they'd been a lure. Bait.

It explained everything Selena had questioned. Why February. Why let them catch up time and time again. Why kill Steve. Hard to lay a trap if someone informed the police about it.

But Axel couldn't dwell on that. They hadn't made mistakes. They'd fought with the information they had. Now they had more. And now they would end this.

He glanced at Selena. She was crawling across the snow and toward the gun he'd left behind. Good. The more guns on Bernard, the better.

Axel got to his feet in a crouch. He moved to one side to get a better view of how Bernard was using Peter as a human shield. He had a gun to Peter's chest. Peter was still as death. Axel reminded himself that no matter how little Peter was fighting now, he'd saved Selena's life. At peril to his own.

And now Axel would do the same for Peter.

Chapter Nineteen

Selena got to Axel's gun and immediately grabbed and whirled, looking for Bernard. But all she saw was Peter, huddled over a corner. And Axel, a few yards away, looking like he was about to rush him.

Selena flipped on her radio. "Fill me in," she demanded to whoever was listening.

"Axel's going to get Peter out of the way so we can take Bernard out," came Carly's calm reply.

"Bernard's got explosives back there," Aria added.

"Some of the team should fall back," Max said authoritatively. "I've already got Scott taking Leonard to some backup agents, but we don't *all* need to be in the potential blast zone."

"We're a team," Carly said, sounding offended.

"We're not leaving Axel behind," Aria added forcefully.

"Damn straight," Selena said into her unit. Max was the one with sniper training, so if he didn't think there was an angle to get on Bernard, she'd believe it. "Morrow?"

"It's no use," Carly said disgustedly. "He pulled out his earpiece."

Selena cursed him silently, keeping her gun trained on the area where Peter was huddled. Bernard was behind him. She would take him out. She would damn well take him out given the chance.

Axel moved. A swift blur. How he managed to run across the stage making almost no noise was beyond her. Axel lunged, and both Axel and Peter crashed onto the stage, but they rolled—Selena couldn't tell who rolled who—nor could she watch them roll. She had to take out Bernard.

She fired, her gunshot echoing with at least one other. Bernard crumpled immediately.

Max's voice came out over the walkie. "I'm headed in to check the explosives. Someone follow and make sure Bernard is dead."

"I've got it," Axel said. His voice was rough. The man was hurt and still doing all the work. But he was closest to Bernard.

Selena dared look at him as he got up from Peter's still body. Axel stumbled a little, but he managed to push himself back up on the stage. As if he sensed the rising fear in Selena, he spoke as he checked Bernard's pulse.

"Peter's been shot," he said. "Fall knocked him out, I think, because the only wound I found was in his shoulder. He's going to need medical attention and a stretcher even if he does regain consciousness."

Selena moved forward carefully, gun still trained on

Bernard, just in case. She couldn't think about Peter. She had to think about handling this the right way. So no more mistakes were made.

No more people shot. Hurt. No. This would be the end.

"Dead," Axel announced into the walkie.

Selena rushed forward and immediately searched Peter's body for the bullet wound. "Right in the shoulder," she muttered. But she didn't find any other wounds except a trickle of blood from his temple. Likely, as Axel had said, from the fall.

Bernard was dead, but there was no sense of relief. Peter was seriously injured, and there were explosives.

"Status of the explosives?" Axel demanded.

"There's a timer on these," Max said from where he was crouched over the bag of explosives. His voice gave away no hint of if he could handle that or not.

They weren't done yet, Selena thought grimly.

"Carly or Aria or someone with a pack? I need tools," Max said into the walkie.

Though Selena was close enough she could hear Axel and Max without the walkies, Selena barely registered their words. She did what she could, used what she could, to put pressure on Peter's wound. But his head was bleeding too. There wasn't anything she could do about that.

It was over, but it didn't feel over. Especially as Carly and Aria rushed forward. Aria dropped a pack next to Max, then crouched beside him taking orders to help stop the bombs.

Carly came up next to her. "Here's my first aid kit. What do you need?"

"I wish I knew," Selena muttered, but they worked together to patch Peter up. "What about you, Morrow?" Selena yelled at him. She was still bandaging Peter's shoulder, but she couldn't ignore Axel might have been hurt too.

"Fine," Axel gritted out.

"Liar," she returned. She took the brief moment to look over her shoulder at him. He sat on the stage, Blanca next to him. His face was bloody, both from his previous injury on his cheek and new ones. The bandage on his previously injured hand was a mess.

But Blanca sat next to him, and he rested his good hand on her furry head. Something in Selena's chest eased. Like maybe this was all over and going to be okay.

"Ambulance is on its way, but it's a ways out," Carly said quietly.

"He can hang on that long, don't you think?"

Carly nodded. "He's young and strong. He'll be okay."

Selena held on to that reassurance from her friend, even if that's all it was. She almost relaxed, but she couldn't ignore the fact there were explosives directly behind her. Max was an expert. He would—

But he stood abruptly and jumped away from the bag. "I can't stop this timer," Max said. He didn't bother with the comm unit now. He shouted. "We have to get out of here. As far away as you can get. Now. Move!"

Carly stumbled to her feet, but before she could help, Max grabbed her and was pulling her toward the woods, Blanca running after them, presumably on Axel's order.

Then Axel was on the opposite side of Peter. "Help me get him over my shoulder."

She might have argued that Axel was hurt and she should be the one to carry Peter, but Axel was bigger. He'd be able to move faster with Peter than she would.

Aria jumped next to them, lending a hand, even as Max yelled at all of them to move. They got Peter over Axel's shoulder and immediately began to head out. They ran as fast as they could into the woods, away from the impending explosion.

"You can run faster than this, Lopez," Axel said through gritted teeth, his pace hampered by the weight of another human.

"We're not separating," Selena replied, keeping her pace even with Axel's. If something happened, she… She just had to be here. With both of them.

"Take cover," Max yelled. "Find some cover!"

But before they could find any, the first explosion sounded.

THEY WEREN'T FAR enough away, that was all Axel could think as the explosion reverberated around them. Heat, the tinny sounds of metal falling all about them. The blast of air that had them all pitching forward and hard into the ground.

Peter's weight landed awkwardly on his own head,

which was another rattle his brain certainly didn't need today. The biting cold was opposite to the heat on his back, and as much as he was aware of being alive, he couldn't seem to shift past that one and only thought.

"Cover your hard head, Morrow," Selena bit out.

He listened to her, folding his arms over the back of his head, but also lifted his head to see her pretty much bodily shielding her brother from the flying debris.

It didn't last long. Small bits and ash still floated in the air, but the thuds of large pieces of wood and other things hitting the ground had stopped.

Static blasted out of Axel's walkie, which must have somehow gotten turned up to max volume during his fall. Max's voice came out booming. "Everyone okay? Carly and I are good."

"I'm good," Aria's voice echoed.

Axel fumbled to roll over to turn the volume on his walkie down.

"Morrow and I are still breathing," Selena said next to him. Her voice was calm and cool and like some kind of balm. They were okay. They were all okay.

"Peter needs an ambulance stat," Selena said firmly.

"There's an ambulance waiting, but we've got to get to it," Aria responded. "Are we clear, Max?"

"Yeah. There were a series of explosives in the bag, but all set to go off at the same time. So, there shouldn't be another explosion unless he had more stashed elsewhere, but my bet's on that being it. Biggest concern now is falling debris, but we seem to be past the worst of it."

"We need help with Peter," Selena said. "He's still unconscious. We're not going to be able to carry him ourselves."

"I'm good," Axel insisted. He pushed out of the snow and onto his knees. The world spun, but he could breathe through that. He'd get used to it. He didn't feel pain. Everything was kind of numb, so surely he could get to his feet. But as he tried, the world didn't just spin, it seemed to tilt.

"You're really not," Selena said, grabbing onto him before he toppled over. "And I messed up my knee a bit. Can you guys find us? Blanca? Where's Blanca?"

"We've got her," Max said.

Selena let out a sharp whistle that felt as though it split his head in half. As if on cue, his entire body started throbbing in pain. Instead of letting Selena hold him up, Axel went ahead and lay back down on the ground.

Selena's face swam above him. "Don't you lose consciousness on me too," she demanded.

"Won't," Axel bit out, though it was a close thing. He could feel his vision graying, his body wanting to retreat from the pain. But he fought through it. Selena was here and they were all right. The team was all right. Somehow.

He heard panting, then felt the rough wet of Blanca's tongue moving across his face. He winced, which sent more sharp lances of pain through his body. But he was awake. Alive.

He reached out for the dog, and Blanca licked his

face again. "Not sure that's sanitary." But it was a nice reminder they'd all made it out okay.

"Up and at 'em." Max's voice, then Axel was being hefted to his feet. Things were still spinning, but Max held him upright. Then Carly stood next to him and wound her arm around his waist.

Aria was helping Selena, who limped. Max had moved over to Peter and was gingerly lifting him.

"Bit of a hike," Carly said next to him. "Just lean on me."

"I'm fine," Axel grumbled, but he ended up needing the support as they moved forward. He watched Selena in front of him, hobbling with the help of Aria, Blanca at their heels.

It *was* a hike, and all Axel wanted to do was lie down in the snow and go to sleep. But he kept moving and eventually the ambulance and a hive of paramedics and cops came into view. The medics rushed forward, immediately to Max, getting Peter onto a stretcher.

"Him too," Carly said, and Axel didn't realize she was referring to him until another paramedic came over. The man glanced at Selena. "You need medical attention too?" the paramedic asked.

Selena shook her head. "No. Just twisted my knee. I'll grab a ride in the cop car and get checked out without bogging down emergency. These two are the ones who need an ER."

Axel tried to argue with Selena, then the paramedic, but he was ushered into the ambulance and wasn't too pleased with himself that he didn't seem to have the strength to stop anything that happened. Somehow he was on a stretcher in an ambulance being rushed to the ER.

He didn't need an ER. He was conscious, wasn't he? The pain was bad, the dizziness was almost worse, but he was *alive*.

Axel looked over to the opposite side of the ambulance where the paramedics worked quickly and efficiently on Peter, clearly the worse off between the two of them.

Axel tried to pay attention to what they were saying so he'd be able to assure Selena Peter was okay, but the words kind of jumbled and it took most of his concentration just to fight the gray fog that wanted to suck him under.

The paramedic leaned over him, studying his face. He lifted the bandage on his cheek, poked and prodded, then did something horribly painful to his hand.

"I'm all right," Axel grumbled, trying to roll away from the medic's attentions.

The paramedic shined the light in his eye and kept examining him as if he hadn't spoken at all. "Concussion. Your hand is a mess. You're in better shape than him, but it isn't getting you out of a trip to the emergency room. Good news is, you'll both survive."

Survive. Axel blew out a breath. Yeah, he had a lot more planned than just *survived*.

Chapter Twenty

Selena had lost all sense of time and place. She'd been right about her knee, though. She'd just twisted it, which was good. They'd given her a pair of crutches and told her to stay off it and to go home and rest. It had taken hours, and maybe she should have listened.

But she couldn't. She'd found her team in the ER waiting room. A bit banged up here and there, but mostly just waiting to make sure Axel was released.

Axel. She couldn't think about Axel yet. She had to deal with her family.

She found Opaline in the OR recovery waiting room. Opaline immediately jumped to her feet. "You should be home," she scolded, but she rushed over and nudged Selena into a chair. "You've got to rest that."

"I will. I just had to…"

"He's okay. He's okay. The doctor said I could even go back and see him in a few minutes. He'll recover just fine."

Selena nodded. She'd known as much, but it was good to hear hope and reassurance from Opaline. Then Opaline's arms wrapped around her. "I'm so glad you're okay."

For the first time in something like twenty years, Selena let herself feel comforted by her older sister's hug. She wrapped her own arms around Opaline and just sat like that for she didn't know how long.

"I need you to believe I really wasn't helping Peter," Opaline whispered fiercely. "I didn't even consider it. I just thought if he trusted me, if he thought I *would* help, I might be able to help everyone else." Opaline pulled back, though she kept her hands on Selena's shoulders. Her eyes were dripping with tears. "I need *you* to believe that, Selena, even if no one else does."

Selena took a deep breath. She'd done her fair share of trying to help Peter in this, in ways that wouldn't meet with Alana's full approval, that was for sure. But more… Peter had made mistakes. Mistakes he'd pay for, but at the end of the day he'd helped. He'd *saved* her when her team couldn't.

"I believe it. And what's more, I believe in Peter. He's going to have to go back to jail, no getting around that, but he tried to help all of us. He… He saved my life." And Axel had saved his. Selena couldn't dwell on that yet. "I'm going to fight for him."

Opaline gripped her hands. "We'll fight for him together."

"And you… You saved us too. Finding all that information about Bernard. We couldn't have handled it the way we did without your information. I'll fight for you too. With Alana or whoever else I need to." Selena sucked in a breath. There were so many old hurts, but at the end of the day, they were family. Family who'd try to save each other when they could.

They'd have a lot to work through, but instead of convincing themselves they were all uniquely misunderstood, maligned or not cared about enough, they had to try to save each other. Instead of doing everything they could to protect themselves from all the ways their parents had hurt them.

Selena stuck around long enough to see Peter. He was mostly out of it, but she got to thank him for saving her, and to promise to do better for all of them in the future. She thought he'd murmured his own promises, but it would take some time before he was lucid enough to fully deal with everything.

Dead on her feet, Selena still tried to argue with Opaline, who insisted she go home. But eventually Carly came in and ushered her outside against all Selena's protests.

Once there, Selena was surprised to find it daylight. She'd lost all sense of time. All sense of anything. But when she saw Blanca waiting patiently in Carly's back seat, Selena felt like maybe everything was going to be okay.

Selena crawled right back in there and cuddled with the dog while Carly drove.

"We'll have you both home in no time," Carly said. "I can stay with you if you need help."

"That's sweet," Selena said through a yawn. "But actually… Don't take me home, Carly. There's somewhere else I need to be."

"I REALLY DON'T like being chauffeured around," Axel grumbled.

"You don't say," Max replied blandly. "And here I thought being injured and fussed over was your favorite thing. You've been so gracious about it."

Axel glowered at Max. He knew he should be grateful he didn't have to spend the night at the hospital, but they'd given him those damn pain meds that made him feel fuzzy without *fully* eradicating the dull ache in his head and hand, insisted someone else drive him home, and left him with a list of instructions on how to care for his injuries a mile long.

He was in a filthy mood, and he wanted to be alone. "You're not staying."

Max chuckled. "Wasn't planning on it."

Axel eyed him suspiciously. He wasn't convinced his friend was truly going to let him be alone, at least for the first twenty-four hours, but Max didn't appear to be lying.

He stopped the car, didn't kill the engine, and let Axel step out. Axel frowned. The lights in the kitchen were on. He didn't leave lights on before he went onto an assignment. Weirder still, Max did not follow. Didn't turn off his engine. Just sat there and gave Axel a wave.

They were really going to let him be alone?

Then, breaking through the engine of Max's car in the quiet of a winter country late afternoon, there was a bark, and then Blanca bounded off the porch. Axel stopped midstep and just watched the dog run up to him, tongue lolling out of the side of her mouth.

She circled him, yipping and whining and wiggling happily.

"What on earth are you doing here?" he muttered at the dog, scratching her behind the ears before moving forward.

Max was driving away and Axel had no choice but to step forward. When he reached his front door, it was unlocked. So, he walked inside.

Selena was standing in his kitchen, fooling with something over the temperamental stove. Her hair was a little damp and piled on top of her head. She wore sweats—*his* sweats—and there were crutches leaning against his counter.

"Did you…break into my house? Are you wearing my clothes?"

She didn't even look over at him. "More or less," she replied cheerfully. She looked around the kitchen. "A little sparse, but I like it. It's…peaceful. Be a good place to recover."

"I…"

"I found the instructions you left the animal babysitter and followed them too."

Axel frowned. "He's a caretaker, not an animal *babysitter.*"

"Right, well, all handled," she said with an easy shrug. "I liked the cows. The chickens, though? Mean as all get-out. The horse is a sweetie. You'll have to tell me their names in the morning. But for now, all you have to do is sit down and eat." She put a plate—*his* plate—on the table—*his* table—with a flourish. Said *in the morning* like she belonged here.

It slammed into him, as hard as all the blows he'd received in the last few days, that this was exactly where he wanted her.

"Come on now. You have to be starving."

He didn't know what he was, but he managed to move forward and sit himself at the table. Blanca padded after him, then curled into a ball at his feet, resting her head on her paws.

The plate was filled with spaghetti. That she'd apparently made. In his kitchen. In his clothes. Was he hallucinating? But her crutches were right there.

Crutches. "You're the one who should be sitting down."

She waved that away, pouring milk into a glass. "Too antsy." She set the milk next to his plate, then stood there, all her weight on her good leg. She brushed fingers over the bandage on his cheek. "You got hospital paperwork? You once called me Nurse Ratched—well, just you wait."

She tried to move away, but he slid his arms around her and held her there. Just held her. God, they were both okay, and the relief hadn't fully washed over him until just now.

She stilled, rested her cheek on the top of his head. Then merely held on. "You saved Peter," she said, her voice cracking with emotion.

"He saved you."

She let out a shuddering breath. "He did. I didn't expect it."

He loosened his hold enough to look up at her. "You're not feeling guilty for that, after everything we went through?"

She looked down at him. Brown eyes swimming with emotion. "I don't know. I really don't know… I talked to Opaline. I visited with Peter. I think…things will be better between the three of us. That's good. I've needed that and was too…afraid, I guess, to try for it. Risk it." She shook her head, blinking back unshed tears. "You better eat before it gets cold. We can talk after—"

"I'm glad you're here. And not just for the food. I'm glad you're here. It feels like you belong here." She inhaled sharply. Then she shook her head, trying to pull away. But he held on tight. There was no more pulling away. No matter how tired or injured or hungry they were. "There's not going to be any more of that. We're going to deal, here and now, with this. With you and me."

She didn't struggle to get out of his grasp anymore, but she did keep shaking her head back and forth. "I don't know *how,*" she said, sounding lost. "You think I understand this?"

"What 'this' are you referring to?"

"How I *feel.* I thought I'd come take care of you and figure it out, but it just… I really don't know what to do about it."

He tugged her down and onto his lap. "I know what you can do about it."

"Oh, don't go thinking with your—"

"Stay, Selena. That's what you can do." He pressed his mouth to hers, just a gentle pressure. Just a promise. "Stay."

She searched his face, and he saw what she didn't want to feel. Fear, uncertainty and, yeah, that guilt they both needed to work through. Then she cupped her hands to his cheeks.

"You know you want to," he added, trying to sound cocksure, but it only came out serious. Hushed. "I know you're afraid. I'm not exactly steady on my feet here, but it's what we both want. What we both feel. You know it as well as I do. But we also came through life or death on the life side of things, so let's let the fear go, huh?"

She swallowed, still searching his eyes, still holding gently onto his face. She took a deep breath. "You're really afraid?"

"Of course I am. I know far more what to do with a gun in my face than I know what to do with a woman and a dog in my house. Doesn't mean I don't prefer the latter."

She smiled a little at that. "Okay," she said, in something no more than a whisper. "We'll stay," she said, giving a glance at Blanca, who sat on the floor, looking up at them with intelligent eyes. "That's where we'll start."

"She'd like it here," Axel said. "Room to run."

"You've got a home here. I've been…wanting a home for a long time. But—"

No, there wasn't going to be any buts. "I'm in love with you, Selena. I think I have been for a while now."

She nodded, those tears swimming back. He'd have thought she'd fight them the way she always did, but instead one slipped over. He wiped it off her cheek. It meant more than words, that she'd finally let that wall down, no matter how reluctantly.

"I think I've been in love with you too," she whispered. "I'm not sure I'm going to be any good at that."

"Then let's agree to give each other a little bit of a learning curve, huh?"

She chuckled, but it was watery, then she leaned her head on his shoulder. And they sat there, in his little farmhouse, holding on to each other in the quiet stillness. In the warmth of love, no matter how much they had to learn.

He had no doubt they'd do just fine.

Epilogue

For the first time in Selena's memory, she didn't particularly look forward to the traditional TCD end-of-mission dinner. As glad as she was the mission was over, and Peter and Axel were recovering, and Opaline hadn't lost her job, she was nervous.

Downright *sick* with nerves.

All she could think about was what Axel had said to her back in that cabin, that the entire team would *know*. Arriving together with him and Blanca was hardly going to help matters.

Not that she wanted to change anything. The whole *love* thing had been surprisingly easy to slip into when they were at the farm. It was *here*, surrounded by the people she worked with day in and out, respected and cared about, that she felt strung tight as a drum.

"What do you think they're going to do? Kick you out?"

She gave Axel a look, not pleased how easily he read her. Or at least, she told herself she wasn't pleased, but the more she thought about it—really let herself think about it and not push away the uncomfortable feel-ings—the more she realized it was a great comfort to have someone who understood her when she couldn't verbalize the things churning around inside her.

It was the thing she'd wanted from her family that they'd never been able to give, but now that she had it in Axel, it seemed to help her find the words with her family.

They walked into the conference room, shoulder to shoulder, to find just about everyone already in the room, helping themselves to the spread of food and drinks laid out, likely by Alana's assistant, Amanda.

Selena wasn't sure what she'd expected. Speculative looks. Teasing. *Something.* But everyone just called out a greeting or smiled.

"All hail the conquering heroes," Max said, lifting his cup.

"Team effort, I'm pretty sure," Axel returned, taking the plate Amanda offered him and handing it to Selena.

"Sure, but we were talking," Max said, gesturing to Carly and Aria. "If you guys hadn't wanted to split Leonard and Peter up, we'd all be in pieces on the for-est floor."

Aria nodded. "If we'd kept together, made the cir-cle, Bernard would have been able to blow us all up."

Selena exchanged a look with Axel. They'd gone over and over that moment themselves, but neither had thought...

But Selena supposed it was true. She'd had guilt there, about letting her personal feelings interfere with a case, but in this strange instance… Max was right. It had actually helped.

Selena let out a whoosh of breath. She'd been harboring guilt or worry or *something*. She'd thought it would take time to work through, but in the end… Everything she'd chosen had actually *helped*.

The team chatted, discussed details of the case and Peter's prognosis and potential trial outcomes. Leonard's ranting that cops had ruined his life, much like his brother's same anger, had earned him a trip to the psychiatric hospital. He'd be carefully monitored for a very long time. The mission was well and truly over.

Still, no one stared or commented on Axel and Selena coming together. No one even gave a second glance when Axel absently ran his hand over her hair. Even as Selena blushed furiously, *nothing* happened.

Alana came into the room, and the chatter quieted as Opaline came in behind her. Alana took the silence as an opportunity to speak.

"While Opaline will be serving a two-week suspension, she was imperative in finding the information that led us to understand Bernard's motives. Which gives me full faith that when she returns, she'll continue to be a fine asset to the team."

The team cheered, and Opaline dabbed at her wet eyes. But her colleagues shoved a plate at her and drinks and…

Everything was going to be okay. Really okay.

A little while later, when Selena was filling her cup

in the corner, Carly came up next to her, leaning against the wall.

Selena braced herself. Finally someone was going to say something.

"It's good to see you happy, Selena." Carly patted her shoulder. "Really good." And then she walked off, petting Blanca on her way back to the table.

Selena took a deep breath and turned. Everyone else was eating, chatting. No one acted differently. And they weren't going to. It was simply…accepted.

Because they were a team. Because they were friends.

"Enjoy your win here, team." Alana tapped on the table. "But be ready for the next assignment."

They'd all be ready for the next one. And in the meantime, she'd have a life. With a sister, a brother. With friends.

And with Axel.

Family, friendship and love. All things that had been within her grasp before, but she'd been too scared to reach for.

She wasn't scared anymore.

She was ready.

* * * * *

"I don't know anything," she said. "Why does TDC think
I do?"

"I don't know." Was this an especially bold gambit on
TDC's part, or merely a desperate one?

"Maybe this isn't about what TDC wants you to reveal,"
he said. "Maybe it's about what they think you know that
they don't want you to say."

She pushed her hair back from her forehead, a distracted
gesture. "I don't understand what you're getting at."

"Everything TDC is doing—the charges against your
father, the big reward, the publicity—those are the actions
of an organization that is desperate to find your father."

"Because they want to stop him from talking?"

"I could be wrong, but I think so."

Most of the color had left her face, but she remained
strong. "That sounds dangerous," she said. "A lot more
dangerous than diapers."

"You don't have any idea what TDC might be worried about?" he asked. "It could even be something your father mentioned to you in passing."

"He didn't talk to me about his work. He knew I wasn't interested."

"What did you talk about?" Maybe the answer lay there.

"What I was doing. What was going on in my life." She shrugged. "Sometimes we talked about music, or movies, or books. Travel—that was something we both enjoyed. There was nothing secret or mysterious or having anything to do with TDC."

"If you think of anything else, call me." It was what he always said to people involved in cases, but he hoped she really would call him.

"I will." Did he detect annoyance in her voice?

"What will you do about the lawsuit?" he asked.

She looked down at the white envelope. "I'll contact my attorney. The whole thing is ridiculous. And annoying." She shifted her gaze to him at the last word. Maybe a signal for him to go.

"I'll let you know if I hear any news," he said, moving toward the door.

"Thanks."

"Try not to worry," he said. Then he added, "I'll protect you." Because it was the right thing to say. Because it was his job.

Because he realized nothing was more important to him at this moment.

Don't miss
Mountain Investigation *by Cindi Myers,*
available March 2021 wherever
Harlequin Intrigue books and ebooks are sold.

Harlequin.com

Get 4 FREE REWARDS!

We'll send you 2 FREE Books plus 2 FREE Mystery Gifts.

Harlequin Intrigue books are action-packed stories that will keep you on the edge of your seat. Solve the crime and deliver justice at all costs.

FREE Value Over $20

YES! Please send me 2 FREE Harlequin Intrigue novels and my 2 FREE gifts (gifts are worth about $10 retail). After receiving them, if I don't wish to receive any more books, I can return the shipping statement marked "cancel." If I don't cancel, I will receive 6 brand-new novels every month and be billed just $4.99 each for the regular-print edition or $5.99 each for the larger-print edition in the U.S., or $5.74 each for the regular-print edition or $6.49 each for the larger-print edition in Canada. That's a savings of at least 12% off the cover price! It's quite a bargain! Shipping and handling is just 50¢ per book in the U.S. and $1.25 per book in Canada.* I understand that accepting the 2 free books and gifts places me under no obligation to buy anything. I can always return a shipment and cancel at any time. The free books and gifts are mine to keep no matter what I decide.

Choose one: ☐ **Harlequin Intrigue Regular-Print** (182/382 HDN GNXC) ☐ **Harlequin Intrigue Larger-Print** (199/399 HDN GNXC)

Name (please print)

Address   Apt. #

City   State/Province   Zip/Postal Code

Email: Please check this box ☐ if you would like to receive newsletters and promotional emails from Harlequin Enterprises ULC and its affiliates. You can unsubscribe anytime.

Mail to the **Reader Service:**
IN U.S.A.: P.O. Box 1341, Buffalo, NY 14240-8531
IN CANADA: P.O. Box 603, Fort Erie, Ontario L2A 5X3

Want to try 2 free books from another series? Call 1-800-873-8635 or visit www.ReaderService.com.

*Terms and prices subject to change without notice. Prices do not include sales taxes, which will be charged (if applicable) based on your state or country of residence. Canadian residents will be charged applicable taxes. Offer not valid in Quebec. This offer is limited to one order per household. Books received may not be as shown. Not valid for current subscribers to Harlequin Intrigue books. All orders subject to approval. Credit or debit balances in a customer's account(s) may be offset by any other outstanding balance owed by or to the customer. Please allow 4 to 6 weeks for delivery. Offer available while quantities last.

Your Privacy—Your information is being collected by Harlequin Enterprises ULC, operating as Reader Service. For a complete summary of the information we collect, how we use this information and to whom it is disclosed, please visit our privacy notice located at corporate.harlequin.com/privacy-notice. From time to time we may also exchange your personal information with reputable third parties. If you wish to opt out of this sharing of your personal information, please visit readerservice.com/consumerschoice or call 1-800-873-8635. **Notice to California Residents**—Under California law, you have specific rights to control and access your data. For more information on these rights and how to exercise them, visit corporate.harlequin.com/california-privacy.

HI20R2

**Don't miss the fourth book in the
exciting Lone Star Ridge series
from *USA TODAY* bestselling author**

DELORES FOSSEN

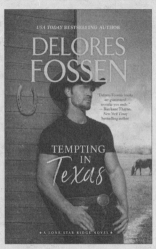

**He told himself he could never be what she
needs. But maybe he's found the only role that
really matters...**

"Fossen creates sexy cowboys and fast moving plots that
will take your breath away."
—Lori Wilde, *New York Times* bestselling author

Order your copy today!

PHDFBPA0221

SPECIAL EXCERPT FROM

HQN

*Deputy Cait Jameson is shocked to see Hayes Dalton
back in Lone Star Ridge. What's even more surprising
is that her teen crush turned Hollywood heartthrob
has secrets he feels comfortable sharing only with her.
As they grow closer, Cait wonders just how long their
budding relationship can last before fame calls him back
and he breaks her heart all over again...*

Read on for a sneak peek at
Tempting in Texas,
*the final book in the Lone Star Ridge series
from* USA TODAY *bestselling author Delores Fossen.*

"I need to ask you for one more favor," he said. "A big
one."

"No, I'm not going to have relations with you," she
joked.

Even though he smiled a little, Caít could tell that
whatever he was about to ask would indeed be big.

"Maybe in a day or two, then." His smile faded, and
he opened his eyes, his gaze zeroing in on her. "I have
an appointment in San Antonio next week, and I was
wondering if you could take me if I'm not in any shape to
drive yet? I don't want my family to know, so that's why
I can't ask one of them," Hayes added.

She nodded cautiously. "I can take you. Are you sure you're up to a ride like that?"

"I have to be." He stared at her. "Since I know you can keep secrets, I'll tell you that it's an appointment with a psychiatrist."

Well, that got her attention.

"Okay," she said, waiting for him to tell her more.

But he didn't follow through on her suspected more. Hayes just muttered a thank-you and closed his eyes again.

Cait stood there several more moments. Still nothing from him. But she saw the rhythmic rise and fall of his chest that let her know he'd gone to sleep. Or else he was pretending to sleep so she would just leave. So that's what she did. Cait turned and left, understanding that he was putting a lot of faith in her. Then again, she was indeed good at keeping secrets.

After all, Hayes had no idea just how much she cared about him.

And if she had any say in the matter, he never would.

Don't miss
Tempting in Texas *by Delores Fossen,*
available February 2021,
wherever HQN books and ebooks are sold.

HQNBooks.com